Cecile

Also by the author:

Eye Of A Hurricane

Cecile

STORIES BY
RUTHANN ROBSON

Firebrand
Books
Ithaca, New York

Several of the stories in this collection have appeared previously in the following anthologies and periodicals: *Common Lives/Lesbian Lives, Evergreen Chronicles, If I Had A Hammer: Women & Work* (Papier-Mâché Press), *Lesbian Bedtime Stories II* (Tough Dove), *Other Voices, Silverleaf's Choice: Lesbian Humor,* and *Women's Review Of Books.*

Book and cover design by Betsy Bayley
Cover illustration by Jane Evershed
Typesetting by Bets Ltd.

Printed on acid-free paper in the United States by McNaughton & Gunn

Library of Congress Cataloging-in-Publication Data

Robson, Ruthann, 1956–
   Cecile : stories / by Ruthann Robson.
     p. cm.
   ISBN 1-56341-002-8 (acid-free paper) : — ISBN
1-56341-001-X (pbk. : acid-free paper) :
   Lesbians—Fiction   I. Title.
PS3568.03187C4   1991
813'54—dc20   91-29775
                                               CIP

Contents

Life is not a (Western) drama in four or five acts. Sometimes it just drifts along; it may go on year after year without development, without climax, without definite beginnings or endings. Or it may accumulate climax upon climax, and if one chooses to mark it with beginnings and endings, then everything has a beginning and ending.

Trinh T. Minh-ha
Woman, Native, Other

Marbalo, Lesbian Separatism & Neutering Male Cats

Marbalo is Colby's pretend friend and sometimes visits with Colby's pretend father.

Cecile pretends that when Colby reaches the right age—sometime substantially in the future—one of us will be able to explain donor insemination to him in such a spiritually scientific manner that he will have an eternally enlightened attitude toward life, or at least not be bitterly confused.

I try to avoid pretending. It's not that I'm an ethicist about it, unless ethics is a synonym for fear. I'm afraid that I could become addicted to pretending faster than to cocaine. First, I'd start pretending that Colby is a darling daughter; that Marbalo is the twin sister; and that both of these kids have the perfect mixture of creativity and obedience, as well as possessing innate knowledge of sperm banks. Then, I'd pretend that Cecile is a lesbian angel who never gets grumpy enough to tell me that I'm irritating her by kissing her on the neck while she's trying to get dressed, and who cheerfully cleans up cat puke. I'd pretend that we all live in a two-bedroom cedar A-frame house on eight-foot pilings in the middle of the woods/on the edge of the ocean/on the crest of a mountain. I'd pretend I have a great job where I work only with the wonderful women of our community, who are consistently loyal, funny, and happy, and everyone appreciates me so much that I only have to appear for morning coffee gossip—and of course I get paid fantastically. If I started pretending, I wouldn't know how to stop. My pretend world would get so perfectly boring that I'd have to pretend to move from Miami to Minnesota so that I'd have pretend problems, like finding a preschool co-op for Colby and Marbalo and buying jackets with mittens attached to the sleeves. I prefer my pretend problems to be concrete.

Cecile knows, though, that I can't always avoid pretending. Actually, I pretend a lot. Cecile is always accusing me of being a closet pretender.

"I'm not in the closet about pretending," I tell her, "or anything else for that matter."

She tells me it's time for me to be in the bathroom giving Colby his bath. The bath is my task. Cecile is the bedtime storyteller.

I wash Colby's reddish curls every night, to which Cecile objects, but not enough to hunch over Colby while he splashes her. Cecile thinks that in thirty years, when Colby is in some twenty-first century therapy, he won't bemoan his lesbian co-mothers and his nonexistent father but will relive the terrors of a barbaric ritual of nightly hair washing. I like to think Cecile is right.

She just may be right if Colby's screaming tonight is any indication. It seems I've gotten shampoo in Marbalo's eyes.

"But I wasn't even washing Marbalo's hair," I explain in my best patient co-parent voice.

"Yes you were," Colby cries. It is hard to formulate justifications for pretend transgressions. I try the remorse and restitution tactic.

"I'm sorry. Let's see if we can rinse the shampoo out of Marbalo's eyes."

"Marbalo will drown."

"No, she won't."

More water. More screaming. Some cream rinse, including a dab for Marbalo's tangles.

Colby and Marbalo dry off. Colby and Marbalo brush their teeth with their matching lavender toothbrushes, one of which I use to clean the amethyst ring Cecile gave me one anniversary. Then Colby and Marbalo stand on the Health-o-Meter digital scale. Marbalo weighs in at her usual double zero. Colby makes the numbers stop at thirty-four.

It's taken him four years, but he's finally reached the amount of weight I gained when I was pregnant. I guess I actually expected him to be about thirty pounds at birth and allow me to lose the other four pounds gracefully, in about a week.

It was all Cecile's fault, of course. When I was pregnant she stuffed me with broccoli drowning in cheese sauce and oranges. This combination had some sort of ultimate vitamin factor, at least according to Cecile. I ate it so dutifully, I expected the baby to be green and orange. I also expected a girl. Girls ran in our families and in our politics. We didn't even have a boy's name picked out. So, while the incredibly heterosexual midwife was pretending it was business as usual, Cecile was rummaging through the refrigerator, thinking quickly. She came back with the name Colby.

"At least the cheese in the refrigerator wasn't Muenster," she'd say later. Sometimes Cecile thinks she is funnier than she is.

When the midwife left, packing her fetascope, her aspirators, her blue cohosh, and the vital statistics certificate with the empty space under *Name of Father* (to be filed in the same building as the Division of Motor Vehicles), we looked at Colby and cried.

What were two dykes going to do with this miniature emissary from the patriarchy who had invaded our lives? One of us would be the one to give him a bath every night. The other one would be telling bedtime stories.

I can hear Cecile from the hallway: *Once upon a time, in an Amazon Land, far, far away, lived a bunch of strong, wonderful women who were always loyal, funny, and happy. They made beautiful weavings from cat hair. One little boy, named Cheddar, lived with them....*

Lesbian separatism is an ethical/moral/political/social practice/theory/vision/lifestyle in which lesbians devote their considerable energies, in so far as it is possible, exclusively to other lesbians, or in some cases, exclusively to other women.

In my postpartum paranoia, I became convinced that Cecile would leave me. Even if it had been a joint decision, even if I had become the "natural" mother because I'd gotten pregnant first, I somehow had the ultimate responsibility for the misunderstanding that resulted in this male child. I kept thinking of all the concerts from which we'd be excluded, all the radical conferences where we wouldn't be welcome, all the women's land on which we could never live.

Until Colby, Cecile and I had been loyal lesbian separatists. However, my breasts filled with milk to feed a ravenous baby boy weren't the only indication that Cecile had always been a little more loyal. I've always thought it was easier for Cecile to be more separatist because she'd been married—only for six months when she was seventeen—but married is married. Now she works with a lesbian collective facilitating cultural exchange between North American and Latin American lesbian artists. She says it's exciting work. The pay is pure puke.

The pay is much much better at the Dade County Division of Motor Vehicles, where I work. So far, the highlight of my career—apart from winning the administrative hearing to get maternity benefits even though I was unmarried—is one man's license plate: he wanted to pay the extra fifty-dollar fee so that his Florida tag could read COCAINE. My male supervisor originally rejected this request, but I convinced him to authorize it by pointing out that if someone was stupid enough to advertise his tastes to law enforcement officials, the county should not intervene.

My supervisor laughed, called me a pragmatist, and approved the request.

Later I found a white envelope with my name typed on the outside and a hundred-dollar bill folded on the inside. I think I used that money to buy sperm.

Cecile did not leave me. In fact, she said the thought never entered her mind. In fact, she said she thought that I might leave her.

Instead, our friends left us. Even our most loyal friends.

Inez said she could no longer come to meetings at our house because our rooms exuded maleness.

Raquel told us she couldn't believe we simply didn't give up the "male-child" for adoption when the "bourgeois were starving for healthy white baby boys" and it would be so easy for us to start over.

Anna gave speeches about lesbian strength being dissipated, about lesbian separatist ethics, about lesbian obligations to the future, about the inviolability of gender.

A woman with whom I'd refused to sleep on a camping trip to Key West the summer before stood up at the Coconut Grove Lesbian Dance, Meeting, and Pot Luck and proposed a rule that would ban all "lesbians in any way participating in male-energized households" from the group.

That was when Cecile walked up to the microphone. She was smiling somewhat sexily. It's one of the features of our monogamy that I realize Cecile is angry when she smiles that way at anyone other than me.

Before Cecile said a single syllable, Inez attacked: "You are a traitor to your species."

"Oh, come off it, Inez. Don't give me that shit. What about Isherwood? What about Orpheus? What about—goddess save us—Samson?"

"They're cats," Inez screamed, squinting as if she had shampoo in her eyes.

"Not just cats. *Male* cats."

Sure it was ridiculous. Even so, we later heard that Inez had given all her "nonwoman" cats away. Cecile and I became more and more separatist, separating ourselves even from other lesbian separatists.

Neutering male cats can alleviate such problems as obnoxious odors, howling, fighting, and staying out all night, and if cats are castrated at an early enough age, these undesirable traits will never develop.

Cecile and I are discussing Bob over our compulsively routine breakfast of grapefruit and eggs scrambled with cheese and half-and-half. Although Cecile is the one who suggested the procedure, she is the one who has the most reservations. I know she's written some letters about the involuntary sterilization of political women in Central America. She's also just more generally thoughtful than I am about these kinds of things. After all, she was also the one to make the impulsive decision not to get Colby circumcised. She has a theory that such infant barbarism is responsible for males being hateful.

Colby (and Marbalo, I suppose) found Bob in the front yard a few months ago. A little kitten with weird markings, especially on his stomach. Cecile showed me an article in the newspaper about some rare Himalayan cat that had stripes and spots, just like Bob, selling for seven hundred dollars. I doubt if we could get a dollar for Bob, even if we believed animals were property that could be sold.

Bob does look a lot like a bobcat, though, which is why Cecile and I named him Bob. Bob is not named after any actor or writer or artist or visionary or famously flaming male homosexual. Our dog is Stella. Cecile and I are hopelessly compatible: we'd never have a cat named Colette or a dog called Dionysus. It does make us wonder about the origins of Marbalo.

"O.K. Let's get Bob's balls whacked off." Cecile can be very decisive when she wants to.

"I'll call the vet," I offer.

"Why not the Spay and Neuter Clinic? It's cheaper."

"I don't trust them," I say, abandoning all claims to pragmatism.

"You just have a crush on the dyke vet, old Mary-what's-her-name."

"Don't be stupid."

In fact, I've always secretly suspected that the vet had a crush on Cecile. I figured that the vet would not disparage Cecile the way she does unless she was trying to placate me. Besides, when Colby was born, the vet was less than sympathetic. I heard she said that more scientifically sophisticated women could prevent the conception of a male. Of course, another woman said something similar about spiritual enlightenment, the phases of the moon, and the failure to birth a girl.

When I take Bob to the Feminist Animal Hospital I do have to admit that D.V.M. Maria Lourdes is kind of cute. She's got these great bushy eyebrows that grow together so that her forehead looks like a hawk with a terrific wingspan. Still, no one's eyebrows could ever match Cecile's—all wispy and wild and defiantly vulnerable. Once, long before Bob, or Marbalo, or Colby, when Cecile was on a crying jag about some crisis we've both long forgotten, she screamed at me, "I don't know why you love me!"

"It's your eyebrows," I said.

She smiled like she thought I was kidding.

Maria, the only lesbian separatist veterinarian I've ever known, is being sweet. "I know you'll worry," she says. "I'll call you at work after the operation is over."

I get a telephone call from *Dr.* Lourdes at the Division of Motor Vehicles.

"Everything's fine," she says. Then she starts expressing sympathy about the hard life I have, working with men in a male bureaucratic system. "Cecile," she adds, "doesn't have to do that."

I can hear Maria smiling.

When I get to the Feminist Animal Hospital, Maria is still smiling. She asks me to have dinner while Bob recuperates a little bit longer from his surgery. She tells me she's heard Cecile is terrible in the kitchen and that I deserve a good meal after Bob's ordeal.

I sort of smile myself, in a half-sexy way.

It's one of the features of my monogamy that whenever I smile my special Cecile smile at anyone other than Cecile, I'm actually approaching anger.

I pretend to be flattered by Maria's request. I pretend to be gracious as I decline. I pretend I don't even consider vomiting. I pretend I am not pretending, for I'm afraid if I start pretending, I won't be able to stop.

Maria coaxes. "Well then, won't you at least join me for wine and cheese? We really do have a lot to talk about. It seems we haven't spoken for years. Is Cecile still not letting you out to play?"

At our compulsively routine dinner of egg noodles, asparagus, and cheddar cheese, I resist telling Cecile what's wrong. She'd be sympathetic, but she'd also tease me.

"Let's leave Miami. Let's move to Minnesota." I crave a problem I can solve, like keeping mittens attached to sleeves.

"Can Marbalo come too?" Colby asks.

"We'll see," we say.

Leavings

I want to pretend that Cecile will be the one to decide whether or not we leave seasonless Miami, whether or not we abandon our lives in Coconut Grove and return here only as tourists shopping for overpriced T-shirts. I want to pretend that I am not trying to persuade Cecile, that I am not giving Cecile wanderlust dreams. I want to pretend that this town is not driving me so crazy I cannot bear to stay another five minutes.

I have exceeded my limit by far. I like to move once a year. At least.

Cecile has lived in this area for as long as she can remember.

I can only remember leaving. I never seem able to reconstruct arrivals. Departures, yes. The pain of change. The looking at people for the last time over and over again. The seduction of staying.

I hate to leave but I always do. Always.

Cecile once told me I was a gypsy, a nomad. Then she laughed. "No, I guess not. You have too much damn stuff."

The gypsies I remember had old cars flooded with possessions. What if one wound up in Oklahoma without tarot cards? Or somewhere west of Denver minus the right color scarf? Or in the North-west needing waterproof matches and pink candles? I told Cecile about them.

"Yes," Cecile said, "I guess you're right. But I bet you never saw a gypsy with a carload of books."

In one of those books on the shelves I'd read that all photographers could rise from mediocrity to greatness simply by burning 90 percent of their negatives. I have only one photograph: it is black and white, and I am holding a camera. My body barely fills the narrow mirror. Everything else is a snapshot. I have boxes and boxes of those, especially since Colby was born. I do not want to burn those snapshots. I do not want to be a great photographer. But I wonder if it works the same with possessions: could I move up a class by culling my possessions?

In the houses of the elegant, there is a single framed original by someone whom I would know if only I were more cultured. If their end tables have drawers, these drawers are empty; if there is a desk, it is called a secretary and has a solitary pen on it. I've been in these places. Cecile has taken me to some of them. They make me nervous.

Wherever I have lived—for years alone with a large dog, then with Cecile, and now with Cecile and Colby—I have stuffed the place with secondhand items that I might need someday. And books.

I like to think Cecile has gotten used to the clutter. At least she does not complain about it as much.

I know she will be complaining about it when we move. We've moved around the Grove a few times, once just across the street after Colby was born, and each time Cecile grumbled. She does not think that rows of cardboard boxes are the accomplishment that I do.

I am longing for those boxes right now. I can get them at the Publix Supermarket in Coral Gables. I can start packing Colby's toys, his books. We could be gone by next month. Gone from the sweltering streets. Gone from the vet at the Feminist Animal Hospital who keeps calling me at work. Gone from Cherry Grove, the women's bar where I did not meet Cecile. Gone.

I want to be forgotten.

For a city of its size, the Miami dyke community is fairly small. It has gotten smaller since I gave birth to Colby. Something about him being a member of the male race. And even before Colby, Cecile had made it smaller. Something about her being not dykey enough, or too dykey, or whatever it was. I guess it was that I had already left most of the women there were to leave. I had a comfortable reputation as a one-night stand. Cecile stayed the next morning, and every morning after. I asked her to stay. I would have begged her.

And now I want to beg her to leave.

Not to leave me, but to leave *with* me. Leave this town that has become a TV show, this slick city on the tip of a tourist-trap peninsula.

After she finishes reading to Colby, I am definitely going to tell her. We have already talked about it abstractly. She mentioned going to graduate school. "Apply to Colorado," I told her, "they have a wonderful arts program." I did not know whether it was true or not, but I thought it probably was. I later made snide, and what I hope were subtle, remarks about the University of Miami.

I watch Colby floating on the clouds of Cecile's words. The only times he appears so angelic is in sleep and in snapshots. And when he was born. Colby was born at home after a short and easy labor. Lucky for me that he wasn't like me, as my mother repeatedly told me. I screamed in pain for thirty-six hours to be born, according to her, but then when the time came to do it, I clung to her for dear life and the doctor had to pull me out with forceps. I like to blame the medical profession rather than myself for my mother's ordeal.

Later, pressing the flat indentation on my head against Cecile's shoulder, I am silent. Tomorrow, I promise myself. The sickeningly sweet scent of jasmine drifts through the open window. I would close it, but then it would be too hot.

"I can read you like a book, but why do I have to?"

I want to pretend that I do not know what she is talking about but I can't. I can't pretend with Cecile. I just hate that about loving her.

"Cecile," I say.

"What?" Cecile says.

"Cecile," I start again. I want to tell her that I want to leave Coconut Grove, that I want to uproot everybody because I am restless and bored. I want to make it clear I am not bored with her, only this place.

Instead, I start crying and talking about Stella.

"Shit," I sob.

"Go ahead and cry. You loved her. You miss her. We all do."

Shit seems to be the only thing I can say. I repeat it like a mantra.

I loved Stella before Colby, before Cecile. Stella, a Bergamasco, had a disposition as moody as my own. I won her in a poker game when she was a puppy. I was going to sell her and her AKC registration, but I fell in love. With her long knotted coat she was meant neither for apartments nor heat, but we traveled around the South until we moved to an overpriced ramshackle cottage in Coconut Grove. I got a state job and Cecile and Colby. Stella got tumors and operations. Stella got euthanasia.

Deciding to kill that dog was the hardest thing I ever did. Cecile held me then, night after night. I cried so much I started scaring Colby. I talked to vet after vet. I threw endless tarot cards. I kept getting the Tower, usually my favorite *(drastic change ahead)*, but it did not answer my question: Should I take the vet's advice and put Stella out of her misery? Or should I let nature take its course? It did not help that there was a murder trial going on of a Miami doctor who had injected his terminally ill wife with an overdose of morphine. Stella's eyes glazed. I drew the Star card *(passing to a new level; opening to the goddess)* from my round women's tarot deck, the same card I had drawn a decade earlier when I was trying to decide if the inconstant sky of my life was wide enough for a shaggy gray animal. Stella became my star, my goddess. Now she was passing to a new level without me. She was too weak to stand. I called the vet. I carried Stella to the car. I wanted to drive out of the Grove then, to spirit my gypsy companion away as if she were a possession I could protect from the thief of death. I wanted to get off this whole continent.

"Maybe we can get another dog," Cecile says, even though she knows I think it is heresy. Get a new pet when the old one goes. Get a new lover when this one isn't working out. Everything is fungible, a word I learned at work from dealing with insurance agents: *nothing special, replaceable.* If I did not live with Cecile, I would not live with anyone. If I can't have Stella, I don't want another dog. We have Bob, the cat. Bob has been known to act quite doggish.

Still, Colby should have a real dog.

"Maybe when we move to the country," I tell Cecile. I am thinking of Montana, how Stella would have loved the blasts of Canadian air, the open spaces.

"You really want to move, don't you?" Cecile asks.

My secret, if it ever was one, is one no longer.

"Yes," I say.

"Then why don't you say so?" Cecile says.

"I am," I answer.

"Yes, after I pull it out of you. Why do you make me guess and worry and then act like I'm the dentist?"

"I don't know," I answer truthfully. I am glad that Cecile is not given to therapizing. Even I could come up with some tantalizingly neurotic explanations.

"Where do you want to go?"

"Anyplace," I answer again, truthfully. "Anyplace I have never lived," I answer even more truthfully.

"That leaves out a lot of places," Cecile laughs. "How about North Florida? Near Tallahassee?"

"Fine."

"There's a graduate library science program there."

"I'm not sure I'm interested in that." I am afraid Cecile has forgotten that I never finished college.

"No, for me," Cecile says.

"You? A librarian?"

"It only takes a year."

"I didn't know you wanted to be a librarian." I am having a hard time imagining Cecile with a bun and glasses policing what adolescents peruse. Even when I know I am imprisoned by a stereotype, I cannot necessarily escape it. Besides, I had assumed Cecile would be going to graduate school in art, her passion and undergraduate major.

"Look," Cecile says, sitting up on her elbow in bed, "maybe I don't, but so what? I need a job. I can't support us with my Arts Alliance Collective work. I like books. Maybe I can specialize in art books. Libraries are nice quiet places."

"It doesn't sound very compelling to me."

"And what you do is compelling?" I try not to be insulted. I am both smug and sensitive about my state job in the Division of Motor Vehicles. I will probably be promoted soon.

"I want," Cecile says, "to be able to support us. All three of us. You shouldn't be the only one to do that."

"I don't mind," I say.

"Maybe I do," Cecile says. "Maybe I'm tired of being able to draw and talk about feminist art in Peru at parties but not be able to make any money. I could make more working at McDonald's. At least I can try the program. I think I can get some loans or a grant to go. And it's a lot cheaper up there. Colby might be happier. There's lots of land. We could find an old farmhouse outside of town and fix it up. You could transfer at work. There must be state jobs. And maybe you could go back to school."

"When do we leave?" I ask Cecile, although my question gets lost in her kiss.

I can smell the overpowering sweetness of the jasmine growing outside our bedroom window. I miss it already, as I sniff the air, again and again, for the last time.

The Room(s)

I think: walls, floor, ceiling.
Cecile thinks: windows, rugs, paint.
I think: confinement.
Cecile thinks: creative opportunity.
Sometimes I think: safety.
Cecile always thinks: colors.

Cecile thinks I'm a little drastic, or perhaps even a little crazy, when I engage in behavior modification techniques with Colby.

"Would you like to spend the rest of your life in your room?" I ask him in my best long-suffering co-parent voice.

"No. That would be a long, long time," he answers. He is at the age where sarcasm and truthfulness are seamless.

"Then," I continue, as if I have already irrefutably proven my point, "do what I told you to do." Or, "Don't do that again." Or even, "Apologize."

He is charmingly obedient. After about five minutes, he asks if he can go play in his room. Cecile lifts her amazing eyebrows toward the ceiling, as if she needs emphasis.

"Besides," she says later, while putting away clean underwear in our top drawer, "it might not be so bad to spend the rest of your life in a room like Colby's."

"Don't say that," I say.

Although I must agree with Cecile, as I almost always seem to, that Colby has a beautiful room. The walls are the palest lavender with four wide windows stretching in a semicircle from west to south. The floors are polished hardwood partially covered with woven raisin-colored rugs. The ceilings are dark and populated with constellations that Cecile spent days researching and rendering, even though the plaster of the bathroom ceiling was snowing into the tub whenever I turned the shower on.

Admitted shower addict that I am, I could not complain. I knew I would love stretching on the bed while Cecile told Colby outlandishly feminist bedtime stories. Cecile prefers to create her own stories, most of the children's books being too sexist for her taste. So far, she has allowed Colby only the bilingual *My Mother the Mail Carrier/Mi mamá la cartera* and the male-authored *Nimby: An Extraordinary Cloud Who Meets A Remarkable Friend*. While Cecile reads or spins her own tales, I look at the stars almost as much as Colby would, perhaps more. With Colby's new double bed (our old bed, now that we had finally splurged on a queen), it was even easier to imagine that I still shared some of Colby's enthusiastic innocence. In this twilight world, with the stars staying exactly where the map prescribed, I could have all of the advantages of childhood with none of its liabilities: I could even get out of bed and have a cup of coffee if I wanted.

It isn't that my own childhood was particularly harsh or unpleasant or comfortlessly devoid of stars. My mother read me bedtime stories with her misplaced accents and contradictory pronunciations until I could read them for myself, and then she let me keep the light on unfashionably late. There was a shelf over my narrow bed supporting such pictorial classics as *The Big Golden Book of Scandinavian Folktales*, *What Every Child Needs To Know About: The Universe*, and *Ballerina Stories*.

Behind my precious bookshelf, which also held my dead aunt's camera and her never-used English watercolor set, the walls were papered with the bold aqua stripes featured in the 1960 Sears catalog. The floors were beige linoleum, a word neither my mother nor I could pronounce, stamped with a gold, red, and arguably aqua pattern of swirls and flecks. The ceiling shrunk away from a spaceshiplike light fixture powered by three one-hundred-watt bulbs.

Even at the time I thought my room was ugly. Even then I knew I did not want to spend the rest of my life there, although no one ever asked me. I wanted a door that would close, a space where I could not hear every movement in the other rooms of the apartment, somewhere I could invite one of the women from my books or my imagination. Even at the time I knew I would go with the first person who asked me.

Monique was not her real name. She said she was from Norway, but she was from New Jersey. She said she was a dancer, and in a way she was. She was like a character from a poorly translated pornographic novel, as beautiful as my imagination, and gave me a room larger than my mother's kitchen. She dyed her hair Winter Wheat, shaved her eyebrows and penciled in drama, and always wore either sandals or boots. She practiced being pale. It would be easy to say I loved her, easier to say I did not.

I lived in my room, in her apartment, for years. I attended school irregularly. I read *Moby Dick* and Plato's *Symposium* for school, and Stendahl's *The Red And The Black* for her. She liked me to read aloud to her with my best attempts at a French accent before she smoothed her hands across my body and raked her fingers inside me. I flunked Interior Design because my monochromatic color scheme for my future house was black, a noncolor according to my British teacher. I charmed my way into a photography course and let the teacher feel my breasts as he lectured me about proper contrasts. I had a fight with Monique because I would not paint my nails red. I attempted compromise by painting them clear. Monique pouted until I borrowed Crimson Desires from the top of her dresser.

Then, for a reason only attributable to an unrecordable shift in the universe, I refused to do something Monique asked me. I said, "Not again." I said, "No more."

She asked me again—nicely, petulantly, severely. I said, "A private room doesn't mean everything." I said, "Just because you touch me sometimes, don't think that means anything." I said, "I hate you. I hate my room. I hate this house."

Then she said, "Just this once." Then she said, "We need the money." Then she said, "It's not like you're not good at working the streets." Then she said, "I'll watch you." Then she said, "I love you."

I said, "I'm leaving."

I thought she would try to stop me, but she just stood there, nodding her head. She clicked her sandals into her bedroom, and I followed her. She stooped to the bottom drawer of her dresser and gave me a white envelope with my name typed on the outside and a smooth sheaf of ten-dollar bills on the inside. I stuck the envelope in my shirt and childishly flounced down the hall to what would no longer be my room. I could hear Monique on the phone telling someone I was crazy as I cried and packed a cardboard box with my dead aunt's camera, a pair of Swedish silk underpants with a heart-shaped crotch, Stendahl, a few men's V-neck undershirts, and three pairs of Levis.

When I came back, embarrassingly ready within a week for any man—nice or not—if it meant Monique would stroke me and say she loved me again, she was gone. I heard that she had moved, and this much was true. I heard that she had married, that she was living on Eighth Street with a young girl from Finland, that she had committed suicide, that she was stripping at The Blue Room. I searched and found out that none of this was true. The only other clue I had was the universe: that's when I rented the room.

The room had walls, a floor, a ceiling. The walls may have been beige. The floor supported a cot that supported my back. The ceiling was a stage for insects.

The room came with a breakfast of scrambled eggs, toast, and coffee without sugar. The room opened into a hallway which emptied into seven other rooms, a bathroom, and a mirror. The room had a door that almost locked.

Behind the desk of the so-called women's hotel that witnessed an amazing number of male trespassers lounged the clerk, a blonde with a scar through her eyebrow. I had crossed my name off the envelope of tens, handed it to her, and asked how long I could stay. She had counted the bills and licked the lead of the yellow pencil before she smeared it across a small pad in attempts at long division. Her final pronouncement had been 117 days.

"Let me know when they're over."

"Don't die up there." She had smiled as she said it.

I had tried to smile back. My mother raised a polite child.

I had no intention of dying. I had no intentions.

It was a blonde white woman, but not the same one, who came to tell me that if I wanted to stay another day, I would owe more money. I thanked her through the door. I got up from the cot and dressed in too-large clothes that did not match the season. I took my underpants and my dead aunt's camera into the hall. I looked into the mirror and photographed myself holding the camera: a white almost-woman who looked like a white boy with fashionably stringy hair. I studied my reflections and refractions as if to prove I still existed. I went to the bathroom and carefully hung the underpants on the sink's cold water faucet. I walked downstairs and into the street.

Then I walked back in.

When I became the night clerk, I got a different room. This one was smaller and in the basement. The walls were painted an industrial green; the floor was concrete; the ceiling was tiled. After work, I had breakfast. After breakfast, I took a shower. After a shower, I locked my door and slept more deeply than I had since I'd left my childhood bedroom. I got paid and walked to Woolworth's. I bought a picture calendar for the wall. I turned it to June, and there was a field of some crazily purple flowers. I bought a straw mat for the floor. I bought a lightbulb for the ceiling fixture. I sat at the counter and ordered peanut butter pie, and then a hamburger and french fries, and more and more sweet coffee. I got paid again and walked to Sears. I bought jeans in the girls' department and sneakers in the boys' department. I got paid again and again and again. I telephoned my mother on my birthday and told her I loved her. She hung up on me. I got paid. I got fired and rehired.

My girls' jeans got too small and my hips remembered themselves. A white woman in red shoes flirted with me, and I flirted back. When she asked me to go with her, I didn't. I quit when I got a job in a camera shop. I took my things to a supply room behind the darkroom and slept on a mattress. I telephoned my mother, and we talked. I learned to develop film. I slapped the owner of the camera shop when he tried to slip his hand in my undershirt. He laughed and did not fire me.

The photograph is framed in five-by-seven aluminum and hangs in the hallway between Colby's beautiful bedroom and the miracle Cecile and I have as our bedroom. Before we moved the picture from Miami to Miccosukee, somewhere among seemingly hundreds of cardboard boxes filled with our accumulated possessions, it also hung in the hallway between the bedrooms. Cecile sometimes remarks that it's hard to believe that narrow person in the photograph is really me. Other times Cecile says that she's simply crazy about that picture and that I missed my calling as a photographer.

I tell Cecile she's missed making lots of money as an interior designer. My only imagined solution to the room that became our bedroom was a well-placed meteor. But Cecile stood in the center of it, looked around and down and up and around again. I could tell she was thinking pretty hard by the way her eyebrows hugged each other.

After Cecile stripped the wallpaper, sanded the floors, and spackled the ceilings, we investigated all the paint departments within a fifty-mile radius. At Handy City, Colby ran through the aisles of nails, mirrors, plumbing fixtures, and sanders while Cecile pondered the relative virtues of Glidden's Thistle (too bright), Arbutus (possible), Larkspur (too pale), Bridesmaid (which I was against merely because of the name), Jubilee (too orange), Arabian Night (too lavender), and Damsel (possible). But then we had to drive thirty miles to compare Glidden's color strips with Sears' rectangles of color supposedly derived from flowers: Aster, Carnation, Rose Petal, Pompon, and Geranium, and then onto the discount stores with their own similarly misnamed products. I had thought that once we had decided on pink (or once Cecile had convinced me that the only possible color for our room was pink), the rest would be easy. I never imagined pink had so many possible hues. I never imagined that we could have such nearly passionate discussions about latex flat wall paint.

By the time we decided upon Scheherazade, Glidden #00402, it would have been petty to point out to Cecile that we should have selected it on our first trip rather than run all over three towns and back twice to Handy City, where the clerks were beginning to recognize us. We bought two gallons, but underestimated because it took three coats to cover the dank walls. I volunteered to make the twenty-mile drive; the paint smell was making me nauseous. I came back with a few gallons of Red Devil High Gloss Polyurethane. Cecile complained about the price, saying we could have gotten a better deal elsewhere. She seemed pleased anyway. After six coats, the floor looked like a wooden mirror.

We argued over the ceiling. I wanted pink, I mean Scheherazade. It seemed so much easier. Cecile told me that anyone who knew anything would know that the ceiling had to be white: a white ceiling makes a room look bigger and more peaceful. Cecile tried to tempt me with a white combination ceiling fan/light fixture. I argued against Cecile's plan because it meant we had to tape the tops of the walls to prevent them from being flecked with white, especially since we had not taped the ceiling.

We taped the walls. In my defeat, I managed to splash a little white onto them. Cecile said she would finish the ceiling herself. She waited, rather patiently, for me to compliment the ceiling and say yes, I did think white made the room look bigger and more peaceful, before she connected the fan.

But I will not begrudge it—our room is a haven. When the sun rises, it shines in the east windows and through the three hanging prisms, splaying fractured rainbows on walls as deeply pink as the inside of Cecile. The sunlight reflects on the floor and refracts on the ceiling.

We open our eyes. We open each other. We open ourselves.

On such mornings, desire shifts the stars inside our heads into endlessly enticing patterns. Cecile's skin glows with the room; my tongue glows against Cecile's skin. Her eyes bulge with blue explosions. I swear I could spend the rest of my life in the perfect universe of this room if only Cecile would get up and bring back two cups of heavily sugared coffee.

Then, there are the other mornings—the other nights and the other afternoons—when Cecile does not want to make love and I do; or when Cecile wants to kiss and I want my mouth and legs closed; or when we both are having fits of passion but Colby wants to chase the rainbows around our room with his Tonka bulldozer (a present from my mother). There are times when Cecile says, "I'm just grumpy," or when I say, "I'm in a funk," or when Colby incessantly kicks at his once-white bedroom door.

Sometimes I think the universe gets skewed. That's when I trap myself in the room. The Scheherazade walls turn mutely beige; the shining floor shrinks under the bed; the ceiling fan waits to guillotine bugs. I flatten myself against a corner of the queen. I do not wish I were dead, or somewhere else, or even someone else. I cannot wish. I cannot imagine a woman, any woman, not even Cecile, who might come and tell me that the time for such craziness is long gone.

When Cecile does slide next to me, she does not say anything. She knocks with her index finger against the hard bone where my eyebrows almost meet. She massages my hands and then pulls us up, out of the bed, out of the room, out of the house.

We stand in the yard, where Colby may or may not be chasing Bob the cat. The fence is laced with fuchsia thread to keep away rattlesnakes. The ground is spotted with topsoil-covered bahia grass seeds. The sky-blue sky is populated with three nimbus clouds crazily behaving like shooting stars.

Taxonomic Classifications: Butch/Femme & Rattlesnakes

When Cecile studied biology in college, she memorized the categories used to classify life: kingdom, phylum, class, order, family, genus, species, and subspecies. I imagine her scrawly, loopless handwriting dutifully recording the notes from the board under the word *humans*: kingdom—animalia; phylum—chordata; class—mammalia; order—primates; family—hominidae; genus—homo; species—sapiens. But I also imagine her silent rejoinder to the professor's conclusions. For the collegiate Cecile, women (perhaps womalia) comprised a distinct queendom, or at least a separate species. Lesbians (lesbialia?) were the most highly evolved form.

Cecile and I sometimes sit on the porch drinking coffee and watching the sun come up as we discuss the divisions in lesbialia. In the early morning, we talk about racial, ethnic, class, geographic, body, and language distinctions. We refer to political lesbians, bar lesbians, professional lesbians, closeted lesbians, jock lesbians, and not-yet lesbians. We wonder whether the butch/femme classification we hear so much about is more mythic than real. Our ramblings are as leisurely as they are subject to interruption. Sooner or later, the four-year-old Colby will wander to the screen door in pajama bottoms too high above still sleep-curled toes and ask for a sip of coffee. He is the reason Cecile has trouble with her lifelong conviction about males being at least a different species. She lifts him up and kisses him; he wipes his mouth off on his pajama top.

One morning, the clouds of summer shifting around the sun, Colby sits on Cecile's lap while we talk.

"Butch/femme is just another way to classify relationships," I say, thinking this is an end stop to this conversation rather than a repeat sign.

"Lesbians always have to classify everything," Cecile sighs.

"Everyone does."

"Who else?"

"Everybody. Plato."

Cecile groans.

"No, really," I say. "There's this whole section in Plato's *Symposium* about lover and beloved, and what it means, and how this is some basic distinction."

"And you believe a bunch of faggots?" Cecile retains the biases of students who fulfilled their math requirement with calculus rather than logic.

"Don't say that. But it's no different from butch/femme. Or from what my mother always said: 'In every relationship one person always loves the other more.' "

"Do you believe that?" Cecile's follow-up question—*Us?*—tries to hide behind her blue-as-after-storm eyes.

"I don't think it has anything to do with feelings. Who really knows what those are?" I had a course in Epistemology. "It seems to me that it's all socially constructed." I also took the Philosophy of Post-Marxism. "Some people have permission to express love in different ways." This must be sociology.

"Just like the rattlesnake has permission to express love with poison?"

Rattlesnakes are probably Cecile's least favorite subject, so she brings them up all the time. Cecile can climb a fifty-foot pine to get the cat down, or single-handedly take the engine out of the car. But Cecile pales and shakes when she sees, hears, dreams, or thinks rattlesnakes.

"Rattlesnakes are just another animal," I tell Cecile. I know she does not believe me. Her college biology can only take her so far.

"They are not so different from us," I continue philosophically. "Kingdom—animalia; phylum—chordata; class—reptilia; order—squamata; family—viperidae; genus—crotalus; species—adamanteus." I expect Cecile to be as impressed with my feat of memorization of the classifications for the diamondback rattlesnake as I am, but she only grimaces. She refuses to comment on my probably faulty pronunciations. She does not attack my conclusions of similarity based on identity of two of the broadest categories out of seven possibilities, not including subspecies.

"How can you say that?" she finally speaks, "when rattlesnakes don't even have ears?" Sometimes it is obvious that Cecile is a feminist rather than a scientist.

Cecile's ears are femme. We had decided this the second time her piercings became infected. She has three holes in her left ear: two are scarred; all are filled with silver hoops. In her right ear she also has three holes, but these are more or less concentric and support a single dangling earring which changes daily. Every night, Cecile takes out all her earrings and swabs the holes with alcohol. She even does this when we take Colby camping, all the while teasing herself about being femme. What she means by this is frivolous, careful, compulsive, silly, somewhat self-conscious, childish.

Colby clamors for breakfast. Cecile makes pancakes, standing shirtless by the stove in ripped blue jeans and cowgirl boots. She uses vanilla, eggs, sour cream, and, I suppose, flour and milk. I get dressed for work in peach rayon slacks and a matching shirt with epaulets.

I went to a state college on a merit scholarship and now I work for a state agency earning merit pay. My job is not political, but it has a biweekly paycheck and benefits. Although Cecile does not qualify under my insurance plan, Colby does.

Only my mother is proud of my work. She takes it as her own personal achievement. When I was a child, she sewed ruffles on men's formal shirts in a factory. She would tell me over and over that I should learn to type so I could work in an office where there might be a window, better hours, and more chances to meet a halfway-decent man. In my mother's system of classification, men were practically a different species and their most highly evolved subspecies was *halfway decent*, characterized by an ability to take care of a wife. In my mother's dreams for me, I needed someone to take care of me. In my mother's dreams, her tomboy daughter was femme.

I never did learn to type until I quit college. In my baby butch determination to thwart both my mother and the state, and feeling rather cocky that I had survived high school and a disastrous multifaceted affair with Monique, a woman twice my age, I decided to major in something exquisitely useless. I enrolled in the English degree program, assuming that four more years studying a language I already knew was feckless at best. When my freshman advisor tried to steer me into the sciences by opining that the only degree more worthless than English was philosophy, I promptly signed up for Introduction to Western Thought. I studied Aristotle's classification system, based upon similarity of appearances, habits, and origins. It was not so different from my mother's system, or from the system of any other woman I've ever known.

When I first met Cecile, I had two friends—Liz and Betty—who were lovers. They both told me that my budding relationship with Cecile was doomed to a quick withering. Betty (or perhaps Liz) said that Cecile was not butch enough for me. Liz (or Betty) said that Cecile was not femme enough for me. Betty and Liz launched into one of their habitual bickering sessions, each of them insisting she was right. They did agree that butch/femme was a good way to evaluate someone else's relationship. They did agree that belonging to the lesbian species endowed them with the power to evaluate other lesbian relationships. Their agreements were not enough to keep them together.

I have not seen either Betty or Liz in years, but I still run home to Cecile. After work, I'm sitting with her on the back porch gulping too-sweet iced tea, sweating in my peach rayon but too lazy to take my clothes off. She wants to talk about the Lesbians with Children support group being started in town.

"It seems like a good idea, at least in theory," I say, as if ideas are rarely theory. "We really do need to know more about how lesbians reproduce."

Cecile is looking out into the blackberry brambles beyond the fence. "No one really knows how rattlesnakes reproduce either."

I hesitate and then decide to try for the delicate maneuver of ignoring this without seeming to. "Cecile," I say, "I'm not just talking A.I. I mean, how do we reproduce ourselves in our own images? Where do we get these images from? Each other? The dominant culture? And where is Colby going to get his images from?"

"I don't know," she sighs. "Children don't seem especially welcome in our culture. Especially boy children. Remember all the shit when Colby was born? It's the only time in my life I wished I wasn't queer."

"Children aren't especially welcome in patriarchy, either," I say.

"It's called heteropatriarchy now."

"Whatever. Children do not fit. Life and love are coupled. Look at Plato's *Symposium.* All that talk about the nature of love and how everybody was once whole but somehow got split and we all run around looking for our other halves."

"Is that damn dialogue the only Plato you ever read?"

"I took a seminar in it. I liked it because at least it recognized that some female halves were severed from other female halves. Plato was the original gay philosopher. Besides, I had a crush on this woman in the course."

"I don't want to hear it," Cecile smiles. She has already heard about randy Randy, as I always called her.

Randy had hair shorter than the male professor's, wore her marine shirt tucked inside dirty jeans, and had a three-inch-wide leather wristband. By appearances, she was butch. Randy smoked Camel filterless, leaned against doorways a lot, and walked like she wanted you to know she was going somewhere. By habits, Randy was butch. Randy came from a stint in the marines, had been a long-haul truck driver of watermelons, and was a daughter to an abusive father. By origins, Randy was butch.

Randy called herself butch, and I called her butch. What we meant by this is: tough, inaccessible, dependable, serious, strong, protective.

In the little-known rituals of reproduction, I was more like her than she would ever be. I had long hair and black fingernail polish. I skimmed the edges of rooms and averted my eyes. I had most recently been a resident of Monique's whorehouse.

But when Randy and I went to bed, I would not take off my clothes and I would not let her touch me.

I kept my clothes on and other women's hands to themselves with most of the women I met before Cecile. I did, however, stop wearing nail polish and start learning to look lesbians in the eye.

"Listen to that," Cecile commands.

It sounds like the sprinkler. The crowded green tomatoes are dry.

"Where's Colby? Where is the cat?" Cecile yells, paling.

Colby is inside, practicing making the letter S with purple magic markers.

"Stay with him," I tell Cecile.

"Where are you going?"

"Outside."

"You can't." She looks like she is going to vomit.

"I can. I've got to get the cat."

"Well, wear my boots."

From the closet, I get Cecile's cowgirl boots. I slip them over my peach slacks. They slide around my knee-high stockings, also peach. My feet have always been femme. I prefer sandals in pastels or satin Chinese slippers. I paint my toenails burgundy. My socks are always softened and match each other.

Cecile sits on Colby's bed. Colby sits next to her. They hold hands.

"Take the rifle," Cecile says.

I hate guns. We got the gun for snakes, but I still don't think that means we have to use it.

I clump into the yard carrying the rifle, trying to track the rattle sound. Out past the fence, in a clearing of blackberry bushes, a coiled ungendered creature of the viperidae family shakes its tail made of keratin, the same substance as fingernails. The cat sits enraptured.

Bob, who never comes when he is called, remains true to his character. I think about shooting. I think it would be a bad idea. I call Bob again.

I go back into the house where Cecile sits on Colby's bed sweating. Colby is telling her it will be all right.

I put the rifle on the kitchen counter. I get a can of Ocean Fish flavor cat food and a can opener. I pick the rifle up. I clump back into the field.

It may or may not be true that rattlesnakes hypnotize their prey with their seductive sounding rattles, but Bob prefers the metal-on-metal of can to opener. I throw can and cat over the fence into the clearing of the yard. I point the rifle at the snake.

"Scat," I say, in my toughest voice, "and don't come back around here."

Afterward, the dark settles around our house, around our yard, around the blackberry bushes beyond the fence. The cat snores on the windowsill. Colby sleeps alone in his bed. Cecile has thrown up and cleaned up. I've taken off the boots and the peach pantsuit.

Cecile alcohols her ears. I pick out sky-blue sling-back shoes for tomorrow at the office. Cecile lights a candle. We slip between the pink percale cotton sheets. I stroke Cecile and tell her I love her. She tells me she loves me. And she touches me. Everywhere.

When The Sky
Is Not
Sky Blue

It was Cecile's idea to rehabilitate the defrost-once-a-week-or-have-puddles-in-the-butter Hotpoint. I wanted to junk it and finance a new one at Sears. Having good credit makes me feel like I survived my adolescence, so I keep a wallet full of charge cards and a state job. Instead of a sloppy wallet, Cecile has imagination, frugality, and determination. She is returning to school after ten years.

Cecile, Colby, and I are in one of our usual haunts, Handy City. Colby is ignoring the bins of nails and screws in favor of pestering us into predicting the exact moment when he will be allowed to go over the fence to primary at the Co-Op Free School. Cecile is looking for our favorite clerk, a white woman with stubborn breasts that poke open her light-blue smock. She is not around today, so we are forced to find the aisle of spray paint without professional assistance.

"Shit, no pink," Cecile says in Aisle 22, as she puts her hands on her hips and spreads her legs apart at a twenty-degree angle. It is a stance I find unfailingly sexy, except when I see Colby attempting to copy it.

"Oh no," I commiserate, not wanting to admit that I had assumed we would be looking for white. After forgetting a trip to Sears, my imagination focused on sanding off the constellations of rust, priming the metal, and giving the old appliance a few coats of white, resulting in the enviable status of good as new. The only refrigerator I have ever known which is not some shade of discoloring white is the gleaming ebony monster in the kitchen of Rose's parents in Miami. The two side-by-side doors do not have to be touched to get ice, water, and another Liquid of Choice, and it has more cubic feet than the bathroom Cecile and I had in our first Miami apartment. Rose thinks her parents' two-thousand-dollar refrigerator is obscene. I am intimidated beyond my credit limit.

In Handy City, I examine the tops of the aerosol cans, looking for lavender, peach, or some romantic pastel. There is only industrial green, red, gold and silver, white and black, two shades of blue, yellow, and day-glo orange.

"I cannot live with a red refrigerator," I tell Cecile. Her clear eyes, watery under the fluorescent lights, are sympathetic but staunch. We will not settle for red; white is no longer possible.

"Let's go somewhere else." Cecile resigns the three of us to another Saturday afternoon of riding up and down the hot roads in search of a fantasy color we will know when we see. Colby sings in the back seat. He changes the words of the rhymes he learned at school (*Humpty Dumpty went to the mall*); he sings commercials (*Wacky Wild Kool-Aid Style*); he mimics the radio (*Stay with me, oh, tonight you're gonna stay with meeee*); he drives us nuts.

"I'm leaning toward the sky blue. How about you?"

"I guess that's the best we've seen." I am sweaty enough to agree to anything that is not red or fluorescent. Besides, I can imagine myself coming home from the supermarket with cheese and broccoli, as well as some white magnets in the shape of clouds to hold up Colby's tempura abstracts and Cecile's notes that always end with *I love you*.

But I cannot visualize Cecile's blue. Cecile and I once went to a workshop on creative visualization: Image-ing Lesbian Utopia. The instructor criticized my verbalizations of my attempts as not well-grounded and overly preoccupied with accuracy. She praised Cecile to the skies.

Anyone can see that the sky, even on this seamlessly hot afternoon is not a single color. In its middle, it is so bright it hurts my eyes: a much too dangerous shade for a refrigerator. Toward the south, it is pale with clouds, though it darkens near the tree line in competition with the newest greens of oak and pine. Around the sun, it is too bleached, like a well-worn bathing suit. None of the shades I can see by twisting my head around the hot car or into the wind seem like the sky blue on the aerosol cap.

In fact, the aerosol cap with the peel-off sky-blue label looks too aqua to be anything but artificial. It reminds me of the embarrassingly wide stripes on the walls of my childhood bedroom. I suggest another brand, another label. We pay cash for two cans of Rustoleum Harbor Blue.

The Gulf of Mexico, with its harbors and swamps, is not far from here, though its waters are more mucky than blue. For me, it is not the ocean. I long for boundlessness, for endless variation embroidered with a white splash of foam or a black shadow of fin. I am one of those odd people who run to the beach during hurricane warnings. I miss the wild Atlantic, the horizon farther than Casablanca.

Inland, I get claustrophobic. The trees here are ancient and advertised as canopies. Sometimes as we drive on the DeSoto Trail toward home, I feel like I am in a tunnel as endless as a night of childhood. The sky is a ceiling I can neither see nor reach. I suffocate under the humid blankets of leaves.

Our driveway veers off that tunnel, inclining past the wall of crepe myrtles and opening into what was once a pasture. The house looks dilapidated, even by rural standards. Yet I feel safe here surrounded by open spaces. Cecile's protection is the flange of trees; she derives protection from camouflage.

While Cecile makes a supper out of bunches of broccoli, I sit in the yard under our bedroom windows, the crystals hanging inside glinting like mirrors bent to send messages. Colby chases Bob, who slides under the PVC lounger, his claws catching my dangling fingers. The lounger is a creamy delicate blue, evenly hued as only plastic can be. The sky lightens into a lonely blue. I know the night will be moonless. Venus flickers in the twilight.

"Are you satisfied?" Cecile asks as she ladles out cheese sauce.

"Of course," I say, not bothering to ask the context of her question. My response would be the same whether she is referring to dinner, life in general, or the cans of spray paint on the counter behind her.

The blue in our house is as accidental as Colby's eyes. There is the quilt that Cecile's mother's mother made with its squares separated by strips of faded Mississippi denim. There is the background in a print of *Two Chinese Girls* bought in a museum when I was twelve. There are the white pots with cornflower designs that Cecile got for her wedding. There is the navy-blue rag rug my mother's mother loomed. And soon, there will be the refrigerator.

I am not a procrastinator by nature, except that I have to be in a certain mood to wield extremely flammable containers with their contents under pressure. The mood descends several Saturdays later. I sand. I spread the newspapers. I read the directions. I *shake well for at least one minute after mixing balls begin to rattle*, grateful that Cecile is not in the kitchen to hear any sounds which might panic her into thoughts of snakes. I try to be steady, but there are drips down the refrigerator's side and on my index finger. I tape the handle and the Hotpoint logo, so as not to spray them. The refrigerator dries into an exquisitely tacky rectangle.

"It's blue!" Colby says.

Cecile is near silent. She compliments the refrigerator without enthusiasm. She takes a shower.

"Let's get the fuck out of here," she says. Cecile believes her premonitions are merely expressions of an ugly mood. I believe Cecile's premonitions are premonitions. I am dressed in jeans and a clean white shirt with the sleeves rolled up almost to my elbows within two minutes. Another three minutes allows me to get Colby into clean blue shorts and a shirt adorned with Cookie Monster playing soccer. I let the cat out. I put our valuables box containing our passports, some jewelry, and bank records into the car in case the house should explode or become host to a shooting spree while we are gone.

Vegetable plates and iced tea at our favorite restaurant seem to soothe Cecile. She is gossiping. She is singing to Colby, "I see the moon and the moon sees me." She is scolding him about using his fingers instead of his fork. She is brushing her hair from around the rim of her ears. She is leaning toward me under the table. She is shining in the twilight.

Cecile drives home with one hand on my leg while Colby falls asleep in the back. I am relieved to find the house in one piece, under a rising crescent moon. Cecile carries Colby into his bed without undressing him. She undresses me instead. She still has her black jeans on as she massages my back, then lifts me up and strokes me hard/soft/hard with both her hands. I turn over for her kisses. I am wet for her, thirsty for her. I take her pants off. I taste her. I promise, I ask, I say words in an untranslatable language. We kiss and touch and sweat until the world apart from our bodies has not yet been invented. Dogs bark outside; the cat jumps on the bed; heat lightning scars the sky.

We sleep as if we are still making love: my right hand is on her left breast; my mouth is kissed on the back of her neck. We are a single creature. But Cecile does not wake when the phone rings. I am the one with the automatic fear that a middle-of-the-night call means something has happened to one of our mothers.

"Let me talk to Cecile."

I want it to be Cecile's brother, but I know it is not. I squint at the clock. It is slightly past midnight. Suddenly Cecile is standing in the kitchen next to me. I hand her the receiver. She is pale and blurry against the hard lines of the blue refrigerator. I go get her bathrobe, but she does not put it on. I touch her arm, but she does not move. She feels cold. Frozen.

Cecile was married when she was seventeen years old to a queer, artsy, rich boy from whom she has not heard for at least fifteen years. After six months of marital bliss, he left her. He moved all the furniture out of their apartment one weekend when she was at her mother's. He did not leave an explanatory note or a forwarding address.

When Cecile told me this story over one of our first breakfasts together, a single tear, vast as the Atlantic, flowed down her left cheek.

I did not tell her then, or since, that I have been as awful as the man who was her husband. Twice. The first time I absconded with all my belongings that my Volkswagon could hold. I told myself I was scared of my lover who drank too many margaritas and once threatened me with a pair of pinking shears. The second time, also without a note or forwarding address, although with a different car, I did not bother to tell myself anything except that it was better this way.

I try not to listen—almost as much as I try to listen—to Cecile's controlled voice.

"No, not much. Really not much in the past fifteen years. I painted a refrigerator blue. I did not go to art school. So, how did you find me?"

I want to scream at Cecile, ME. ME. ME. *I was the one who painted the refrigerator blue. You have done a lot in the past fifteen years. You have loved me. You have lived with me. We have had a child together.*

I realize Cecile does not want him to know any of this, but I still want to scream my existence as a reminder of the woman who answered the phone, the woman who was holding Cecile as close as I do every night. ME. ME. ME. And I want to scream at him, YOU SHIT. *When you leave someone, you leave her to her life. You do not telephone her years later to remind her of the pain you inflicted. When you leave, you stay gone. Forever.*

I am still screaming inside my numbing head when Cecile hangs up the phone. I help her put on her bathrobe, the one I gave her last year with its little splashes of spectrum against a white velour background. Her eyes are blankly blue. Her hand is icy as I lead her outside, because I do not know what else to do.

"Are you all right?" Cecile asks me this as I am about to ask her.

"Yes. How about you?"

"Fine." Cecile could have a body full of broken bones, and if I asked her how she was, she would say, *Fine.*

We stand in the yard, watching the stars shift against the blankness.

"Is that Venus?" Cecile asks, pointing vaguely. The stars of my childhood were double-bolted behind the city skies. It was Cecile who taught me the planets, the constellations. Cecile taught me about binary stars and the classifications of galaxies. Cecile mapped the sky on Colby's ceiling. It was Cecile who explained that Venus is never visible in the middle of the night: the planet is an evening star or morning star, appearing either at twilight or dawn.

"What did he say?" I whisper.

"Nothing. I don't know."

"What does he want?"

"Nothing. I don't know."

"How did he find you?"

"I don't know. He wouldn't say."

"Where is he?"

"Wisconsin. Minnesota. Traveling."

"What does he want?"

"I don't know."

I pull Cecile back inside, sit her at the kitchen table. No tears roll down her face. I make her a cup of decaffeinated coffee. She does not drink it. I pull her back to bed. We hold each other until we fall asleep.

I have almost forgotten about the phone call, although one day I am in the drugstore buying a flea collar and I trip into a rack, scattering cards that read, *Happy Birthday to My Darling Husband.* I drive Colby to and from the Co-Op Free School, convincing myself that Cecile's ex-husband is probably a very nice guy. I still hate his guts. I try not to remember their smiles in the wedding photograph on one of Cecile's mother's walls. I remind myself that the past is past for very good reasons.

The past, however, has other plans. I assume it can only be a parent from Colby's free school looking for transportation when I hear Cecile on the phone at 7:00 A.M. I am still dripping into Cecile's bathrobe from my shower.

"Nothing," she says, in her most tense voice.

"The refrigerator is still sky blue," she says.

"Oh. That's nice," she says, still tense.

"Well, good luck." She hangs up.

She continues making Colby's pancakes, as if she has not been interrupted.

"What did he say?"

"He's getting married. Again."

"I thought he was gay." I stare at the syrup.

"I thought so too."

"Are you all right?" I ask her.

"Why wouldn't I be?" she asks back, flipping more pancakes. She does not ask if I am all right. I do not know what I would answer if she did.

We get dressed. She helps Colby with his yellow shorts and yellow-striped shirt. She makes Colby's lunch. We do not speak in the house. We do not speak in the car, and Colby does not sing in the back seat although it is a thirty-five-minute drive to the Co-Op Free School. When we drop him off, he runs to his friends, glad to be rid of his sullen co-mothers.

"Why," I finally ask her, "did you tell him the refrigerator is sky blue?"

"Blue is his favorite color."

"How can blue be anyone's favorite color? It is so common, so boring. I thought he was an artist." I do not care if I am silly, or if he is a nice guy, or if blue is the best color in the universe. I hate blue and I hate him and I hate the fact that Cecile was married.

"He used to say that blue was the only color that could be both black and white. You know, like when things are so black they look blue or so white they have that bluish tinge." Cecile is heartlessly matter-of-fact.

That Cecile remembers such a detail about this man over a decade and a half later must mean something. But does it mean she once loved him? That she still loves him? That she has a good memory?

The new State Department of Motor Vehicles building looms ahead. "Let me out at this corner," I tell her. I kiss her good-bye. "I'll call you later if I have to work late," I remind her.

I do not go into the office building, but stand on the street looking downhill at the other state buildings forming a corridor. The sky is brilliant this morning, although filled with flat-bottomed clouds like barges on an upside-down sea.

I love Cecile. I love Cecile so much that I want to empty our beautiful home of everything we own so that she will never forget me. I want her to remember everything I have ever said, even after twenty years. I want to throw the refrigerator in the junk pile and pull out the telephone cords and smash those cornflower pots.

It is not a long hike to the mall. At Sears, I charge a Budget Rent-A-Car. It is a four-hour drive to the ocean. I call Cecile from Daytona Beach, tell her I will be home late, remind her to pick up Colby. I wander along the Atlantic. I see men and women holding hands; I imagine them married. Cecile was married, I say to myself. Not only am I ashamedly jealous of anyone who ever knew Cecile before I did, excepting her parents, I am also resentful. In Image-ed Lesbian Utopia, would there be weddings, ceremonies, marriages? Probably not, unless there were vows of nonmonogamy. Still, the only world I can visualize is one in which women cannot marry each other.

In my preoccupation with accuracy, I can picture Cecile's father guiding her down that Protestant aisle. She is dressed in white and looks like an American Princess. I could never have been the one who was waiting for her near the altar.

I could also never have been her. When I was not yet fifteen my mother told me: "Don't ever get married, but if you have to, then elope. I've got no money for a damn church wedding. And there's no one to give you away, anyway." My mother's warning did not worry me. Even then I could not imagine myself with a husband, or with any man.

I go back to the parking lot. I try to visualize Cecile. I wonder what she and Colby are doing right now. I sit in the red rented car and listen to the radio. *Stay with me. Stay with me.* I wait for twilight, for the evening star.

When I get home, Colby is sleeping. Cecile is on the porch with a cold cup of coffee. The old Hotpoint refrigerator is painted black. It is dotted with stars and planets: Polaris, a pink-tinged Antares, Venus, a crescent moon that will never wane.

Minneapolis, Minnesota & Monogamy

Cecile does not love the ocean like I do. She thinks forests are equally awesome. I am the one with the need for the blue wave of horizon where Atlantic and eastern sky join like lovers. So, when my eyes glaze with what Cecile calls my Casablanca look, she suggests that we pack a single suitcase for ourselves and Colby and hightail it to the beach.

This morning we are sitting on Guinevere's porch, on an almost-island straddling the Atlantic and the Indian River, slightly south of the 28th parallel, the demarcation dividing the real Florida from the nontropical parts. She is inside with Colby, presumably making iced tea, but probably engaged in activities secret to their longstanding and quite private mutual adoration society.

"Your eyes look like the ocean," Cecile tells me.

"I was just about to tell you the same thing." Our eyes are actually very different shades of blue, but then again, so is the ocean.

"Can you see Casablanca?"

"No," I answer seriously, "it's too misty." We are also too far south, even if I could see a few thousand miles, but such a detail seems trivial. I have always wanted to move to Casablanca.

Colby trails after Guinevere and her tray of glasses, pitcher of ice and tea, mint and lemon, as if he is a medieval manservant instead of a preschooler who desperately wants to graduate into primary. Guinevere, in fact, looks like a Lesbian Lady of the Dark Ages. She has blue-black hair that shines smooth as raven's feathers and bluishly white skin that she always shields from the sun.

"I feel so sociable," I say, sipping from my tall glass engraved with the letter G.

"You know, you girls should be more sociable." Guinevere calls us girls, although she is only twenty or so years older than either of us.

"You should talk." Guinevere rarely gets out of the hopelessly heterosexual seaside community where she has lived for over thirty years. She grew up on another island, Nantucket, where her mother was both a judge and real estate mogul. Before her mother died, Guinevere worked with the St. Lucie County Division of Motor Vehicles. I met her many years ago when she came to Miami for training and I was the one to teach her the intricacies of title registration. Now, she does not work and I am a supervisor for the Division in the state capital. Guinevere has investments; I have credit cards.

"O.K.," she laughs. "But really, you two should go somewhere exciting this summer."

I do not say anything about being broke.

Cecile says, "We're actually thinking about going to the Women's Studies conference this year. It's in Minneapolis. They're having some workshops that are supposed to be good."

I do not say anything about being surprised.

"Sounds incredibly boring. Both the event and the location. A bunch of flat academics in the flat Midwest." I have always appreciated Guinevere's ability to be blunt.

"Well, maybe," Cecile concedes, "but it might be kind of fun to go to a workshop on Post-Monogamy."

"Like I said," Guinevere says, "it sounds boring."

"The workshop or monogamy?" I tease.

"Both," she says unflinchingly.

"And what would Dot say about that?" I am only half-teasing now.

"More than likely the same thing. Dot and I are just very very good friends," Guinevere laughs. "Monogamous almost."

Guinevere and Dot have lived in the closest of proximities for over twenty years. *Together* would not be accurate, for although it seems to me that Dot spends every night in Guinevere's house—in Guinevere's bedroom—Dot maintains a cottage on Guinevere's property which she rents in exchange for lawn maintenance. I admit to being appalled at what I considered a rather feudal arrangement, until I spent a day with Dot canoeing on the Indian River.

"I am not the marrying kind," Dot had said as we were driving back from the river, the canoe strapped in a way I hoped was secure on the top of Dot's Subaru station wagon. We had not said more than "this way" or "look" in the five hours we had been together, but she acted as if she was answering some question I had meant to ask. "And even if I were, I wouldn't want to rush into anything."

I had nodded in recognition: that's how I was. At least, that's how I had always been until I met Cecile.

Cecile—my everything. Although I did not know that my everything was seriously considering going to Minneapolis. She had mentioned the conference to me, once or twice, but always in the context of it being too far or too expensive or too unrealistic to go.

On the almost seven hour drive back from Guinevere's, we have lots of time to discuss our recent move from Miami to North Florida, the slight but exciting possibility of moving to Casablanca, and even going to Minnesota, while Colby sings, colors, crumbles the crackers, and does everything except sleep in the back seat. We decide not to go to Minnesota; it is probably too cold, even in June.

Once again in Miccosukee, I am ready to go anywhere. It is late May, which in Florida is the middle of the summer. The heat here is unbroken by ocean or rain, and we are too far north to deceive ourselves into the relief of tropical breezes. We discuss vacation time, childcare for Colby, Cecile's project due the day we would return from the conference. We send in forms. We make reservations. We wait for June.

Living almost anywhere in the South means changing planes in Atlanta. We do. Colby is thrilled by the steep escalators, the trains rushing by at two-minute intervals, the moving sidewalks. Cecile is chagrined.

I always think of Cecile as adventurous; I forget her insecurity in new places. So, I hold onto Cecile's hand the way I often do in the world: I put Colby between us and have him hold on to both of us very tightly. The other inhabitants in transit from Concourse A to Concourse C either try not to notice us or give stingy smiles. Finally, we are out of the transportation mall and at our gate. Finally, our plane arrives. Finally, passengers with small children or passengers needing other assistance are boarded. Finally, the plane takes off. Finally, we land.

From the windows of our airport taxi, the grass stretches, flyaway and dirty blond. We are in the midst of a national disaster drought, and the land looks burnt, as if by an encounter with a terrible hairdresser. There are a few patches of garish-looking green, and in this birthplace of an antipornography ordinance, I notice that one of these rare verdant squares is in front of a very polite looking ADULT! ADULT! ADULT! BOOKSTORE & MORE.

The university is also an oasis, though much larger. The lawns are lush and manicured. Our taxi driver, a man who asks us whether there is some big women's thing going on with famous women, finds our residence hall and even helps us drag our luggage onto the curb.

Once inside Pioneer Hall, Colby teetering toward intense crabbiness, the three of us stand in line for our room, only to find out we have two rooms instead of one. I explain our situation.

"Why can't you just let the child stay with one or the other of you?"

Cecile's eyebrows arch in reply like scabbards momentarily sheathing Amazonian swords.

"Because," Cecile says, "we are a family unit. And we expect to be treated as such."

Family is not the weapon I would have chosen. The guard of the room assignments, however, is threatened enough to say she will see what she can do. She does this by going to another cubicle and getting on the telephone.

Cecile looks at me, her eyebrows still curving dangerously. "I'm sorry," she says, "I know what you think about that word. But like it or not, we *are* a family. As much a family as any other family."

"It's O.K.," I say. "I like what we are. Just not that word."

There are many words I do not like: *family, motherhood, paternity, marriage, couple, relationship, monogamy, lovers, partnership,* and *life companions.* All those words seem inappropriate in the universe of Cecile and me. They seem too easy, too diminishing, too empty, too common. They seem like weak attempts to explain something that is too gloriously mysterious to be reduced to an explanation.

At the workshop on Lesbian Theory, which Cecile and I attend the next day after a night of almost comfortable rest with Colby in our college "suite," explanation is as rampant as sweat. In the triple-digit temperatures and unairconditioned rooms women crowd their varied bodies close together. I fight claustrophobia, as one moderator insistently refers to "my extra chairs" and "my fire aisles," and "my front rows," forgetting in the swelter of the moment that even if the chairs, aisles, and rows were not claimed by the University of Minnesota, our community would not allow any individual to be so proprietary.

The close, hot confinement reminds me of being outrageously nine, sprawled in my girlfriend Vera's attic/crawlspace, kissing each other in the after-school afternoons before her mother and my mother came home from work. Despite my claustrophobia, I feel grateful that I grew up to sit surrounded by so many women. It is easy to relax among women. I assume that every woman in this room is a lesbian. It is even easier to relax among lesbians.

Since before I was in the attic at nine, I have looked at women: at the ways they walk; at their hair; at their asses; at that sexy spot on the neck where I first kissed Cecile; at their earrings. Here, with Cecile's hand on my thigh—Colby not between us but at childcare—I am still looking at women, although now I find myself looking only at their hair. I am the one who cuts Cecile's hair and I am always looking for ideas. Cecile's only mandate for her personal hairdresser is that I make sure her hair does not touch her ears.

"What are you staring at?" Cecile asks, almost nervously. She eyes the young woman with curly brown hair and dreamy eyes who keeps shifting in the seat next to mine. I have seen her stepping from the shower in the bathroom on our floor. She looks innocent, either in spite of her eye make-up or because of it. "That woman's hair. Over there," I nudge Cecile. "The one with the labrys shape shaved into her skull."

"Stupid." Cecile sounds sincere and relieved.

"I don't think I could do your hair like that, anyway." I smile at her as if I have known her as long and as well as I have.

During a discussion of monogamy, Cecile and I leave, holding hands, because we need to go get Colby. At the Lutheran Church à la childcare center, Cecile has a difficult time prying our child away from Megan, one of the workers. Every time we have dropped Colby off, he has run to grab Megan's hand. Every time we have come to pick Colby up, he has clasped at Megan's clothes. Colby is acting like he is crushed out.

Outside, with Colby asking when he can go back to see Megan, Cecile scowls.

"I think that woman's a jerk," she says. "Colby seems to love her. And don't think I didn't see her trying to flirt with you when we signed him in this morning."

Cecile is very sexy when she is sullen. Still, I want her to be happy. So I tell her, "Be glad. We are off enjoying ourselves in sweatboxes listening to dykes sounding intellectual. He's having a good time too. Let him be free. Be happy that he's happy, that he's not neurotically dependent on us. Be glad he's an individual."

My speech sounds eerily familiar: I wonder where I have heard it before. Oh, yes. Substitute *me* for *he*, and I have given this rap to scores of women.

Before I met Cecile, I substituted politics for feelings. All my words were slogans; all my slogans were shields. I could disparage whole lifestyles in the way I pronounced them: *monogamy, family, relationship*. I demanded only freedom, which came so hard. I tolerated everything except boredom, which came so easily. If I had a few slogans parried back at me (*fear of intimacy, incapable of commitment, candidate for therapy, bitch*), that only seemed fair.

As we walk back to our suite, Cecile still pouting but not quite as sullen, Colby excitedly points out yet another rabbit. It amazes Cecile that these cute almost-rodents survive in downtown Minneapolis, that the students or the locals do not kill them. It seems logical to me that all the animals would be here: it is the only green place for miles and miles. The rabbits scurry. Cecile wonders how they do not get crushed in traffic.

I am wondering if rabbits are monogamous, knowing the general perception, of course, that they are not. There are myths about animals which mate for life (I once knew a woman who could recite every one, but she wrote poetry. All I can remember is whooping cranes). I am unconvinced rabbits might not be like me; perhaps no one has ever observed a rabbit who met the right rabbit.

A shower with all three of us squeezing into a stall meant for one college student, and a dinner a few blocks off campus, revives us. Another shower allows us some sleep in the solid heat of the night. Cecile even half-smiles at Megan in the morning as Colby runs to grab her hand. We are discussing choices for our next workshop, when Cecile's eyes pull in the grey sky and her tongue pushes past my lips. We walk back to our dormitory suite, where the two twin mattresses are still pushed together on the floor under the open narrow windows. The linen service sheets tangle while all our theories become practice.

Later, still flushed, I sit on the grass waiting for Cecile to liberate Colby from his fascination with Megan. That same young woman who sat next to me in the lesbian workshop now slides too close to me on the short midwestern stone wall. I have eavesdropped on her revealing her rather ordinary coming out story to at least three other groups. She is insufferable, but I suppose we all have been. I nod to her mascara. She smoothes her jeans skirt again and again. I try to recognize myself twenty years ago, but I cannot believe I was ever that perky.

"Don't you just love these rabbits? They are so full of lesbian essence."

I try to smile, thinking Colby has more in common with this woman than I do, thinking of a great name for a perfume which replicates the scent of sweat.

"You're on the same floor with me. Why don't you stop in at my room tonight?"

"Why?" I am older, wiser, more mature and experienced. I will intimidate her vagueness.

"To experience our lesbian natures."

"How?" I am getting nervous.

"By having sex." She is flapping her eyelashes like wings.

"No, thank you." I retreat into politeness, my bluff having been called.

"So, you're monogamous." She is accusing.

This woman, lesbian or not, is a little shit. I was opening women's legs with my tongue before her head even crowned from between her mother's legs. She does not understand a damn thing about monogamy. Of course, I do not either.

I cannot explain Cecile and me, not to this baby dyke, not to any of the women in Minneapolis, with concepts such as monogamy. No, I need a metaphor. A beautifully imperfect metaphor. A mirror.

I've always been shocked when I looked in the mirror. I spent childhood years inspecting them. I spent 117 days in a room without a mirror, coming out only to go to the bathroom, carefully avoiding the cardboard framed mirror in the hall. And I've taken a mirror to my face because a woman I tried to love once told me I was beautiful but then left me for a boyfriend. I created a detailed abstract in my flesh with a splinter of glass. My hundreds of lacerations, like my affairs, did not leave a single scar, at least not one that anyone else can see.

Still, when I look in a mirror now, I do not see any of the elusive beauty that woman saw or even any of the thin lines of crusted red that woman pretended she never saw. I see Cecile. I have looked at Cecile so hard and so long that any other face, even my own, is foreign. And I have touched her and stroked her so soft and so long, that any other body, even my own, would be peculiar.

I guess that's monogamy.

The young woman thinks it is something that can be—and should be—overcome.

"Let's do a threesome, then," she says enthusiastically. "I have always wanted to do one."

I do not tell her that when I was her age, I wanted to do them too.

That I did them, threesomes and moresomes, and I even got paid for some. I do not want to sound condescending. I would rather be uninteresting.

"No, thank you." I fall back, again, on politeness rather than politics.

When the woman sees Cecile, she leaves without a greeting. Though at lunch in the college cafeteria, she waves Cecile and Colby and me over, as if we are her best friends. I think, perhaps, we might be.

Cecile and I look at each other.

"Guinevere told us to be sociable," one of us says.

"Damn Guinevere," the other says.

Balancing our trays of noodles and jello cubes, we walk over to the table of about seven women of various ages and colors. The talk is of sex.

"We lesbians need to talk more about sex."

Heads nod. Colby wants to eat his jello before his noodles, but Cecile is being strict.

"Yes. Our movement needs more talk about what we do in bed."

"Exactly what we do in bed."

"And," a pale-skinned blonde-headed woman pauses dramatically, "exactly who we do it with." She tilts her head as if she is giving a hint that the answer might not be only other lesbians.

"Why?" one woman asks. I like her immediately. She has long blue-black hair and suave eyebrows. She wears a T-shirt that says Asian-American Lesbian Alliance. I smile at her. She smiles back.

"Have any of you read that survey?" The blonde woman takes charge again of the discussion.

"No, eat your noodles first." Cecile raises the level of discourse.

"The one about lesbians not having as much sex as married or gay male couples?" A round-faced woman says this. She is wearing several pendants: a labrys, a Star of David, an Islamic crescent.

"That is really a pity," the young mascared woman sighs. Perhaps she has joined a community which might not be as exciting as she first thought.

Colby squishes the jello through his teeth. Most of the women at the table look away.

"I want to go home," Colby moans. I do not know whether he

means the dormitory or Miccosukee, but I excuse us.

"I'm sick of sex," Cecile says, as Colby holds hands between us.

"I hope not," I smile. She does not smile back. "But really, Cecile," I say, "don't you notice how everyone talks about how we should talk about it, but no one ever talks about it?"

"What?" Cecile stops.

"I mean, in all that discussion, no one said a word about what she—or any other woman—does in bed."

"Are you complaining?" Cecile asks.

"No. I'm just wondering about it."

"Then read some pornography."

"It's called erotica now," I say.

"Whatever," Cecile says. "It's too hot in this place to care about any of it."

Cecile has a point.

"I want to go home," I moan to Cecile later, when we are back on our mattresses on the floor. We cannot get back to our bedroom with the pink-painted walls and the country breezes soon enough to suit me.

The morning after we successfully maneuver our way through Atlanta's transportation malls, I wake early. Colby is still sleeping. Cecile has her mouth half open, as if she is still kissing me as deep as she did last night. I want to make Cecile coffee, and bring it to her in bed. Outside, the yard is shrouded in fog. The sun is almost over the eastern tree line, but the mist persists. It reminds me of Seattle, where I have never been. I think of the ocean there, the Pacific, probably as blue as Cecile's eyes. The forest, I've heard, goes right up to the beach. Cecile would like it there, though she would carp about having to move. Sometimes I think if we could only find the right place, we would never go anywhere else ever again.

What We Do In Bed

One of the most salacious activities Cecile and I perform on our queen-size, in full view of our combination ceiling fan/light fixture, is reading to each other. We do not merely recite provocative phrases from our separate novels or self-help books. We do not read aloud a poem or two which we consider especially intimate. We do not share portions of essays which accurately portray some facet of our experience.

Instead, after Cecile pretends to read our child Colby a story (often substituting appropriate words—there are not too many Read-Aloud Books about co-mothers) and Colby slips reluctantly into sleep, Cecile gets our book.

It is never a classic. It is not a book from the Current Concerns or Lesbian Interest shelves at the small alternative bookstore almost an hour's drive from our bedroom. It is a detective novel.

Tonight, Cecile and I are anxious to spread across our earthy pink sheets, a glass of lemonade on the wicker nightstand on my side, a glass of iced tea on the wicker chest on her side. We are in the midst of a gay male mystery that Cecile found in the paperback trade bookstore, not too far from the alternative bookstore.

The action in this detective book takes place in New Orleans, about a seven hour drive from our bedroom. The first time I was ever in New Orleans was a long time before I met Cecile. I was there with my friend Dulcie, who suggested we trek from our Miami shit jobs to see a Vodun fortuneteller. We hitchhiked up the Turnpike to Route 75, and then across on Interstate 10, passing within five miles of where Cecile and I now live. Dulcie wanted to find out whether her mother in Cuba was dead or alive. I wanted an adventure.

Our Vodun woman was beautifully shrouded in scarves and stones swinging from thin threads. Her skin and hair were darker than mine, but that was true of almost everyone in Miami, is true of almost everyone in the world. Her skin and eyes were darker than Dulcie's, but her hair was lighter in the sense that it attracted and reflected more light in the small alcove.

Mme. Celeste told Dulcie her mother was alive and sewing in Candeleria. At least that is what Dulcie told me the woman said. When I went into the private room off the alcove, Mme. Celeste asked me for a piece of jewelry, although it was not obvious I was wearing any. I was impressed into obedience. I unbuttoned my buttondown shirt and reached into the not-very-mysterious interior of my black leotard. I pulled out a thin silver band which usually swung between my breasts on a dirty string. I handed it to her. She did not smile. She said, "The young woman you travel with is in love with you. You will hurt her, just as you will hurt the many women who will travel with you, most not very far, most for only a short time. But someday you will stop your carelessness. Someday you will be married and have a child."

I had wasted five dollars. Dulcie did not love me any more than I loved her. We were pals. And I could not imagine being married.

"I'm queer," I told her.

"It's your ring," she said, handing it back to me. She continued not smiling.

There are no Vodun women in the detective story which Cecile is reading aloud. I guess a fortuneteller would spoil the plot. The hero could take off his Rolex watch, hand it to her, and hear, *It is a very important man who is murdering all those men in the bathroom of the gay bar. An elected official. Like a Congressman.*

Yes, a Vodun woman would taint the book. Sometimes it seems like any woman would taint the book. There are some women in these pages who either dress fabulously or drably, but however their costuming abilities are categorized, the women are invariably referred to as fish.

"You aren't going to like this." Cecile interrupts herself as she is reading, taking a slug of her iced tea.

"Oh, go ahead."

" 'What did the fish say?' " she reads.

"Oh, shit," I say, "I'm getting sick of this."

"I told you," Cecile tells me.

"What does it mean, anyway?" I ask. Cecile knows a lot of gay male slang. She was once married to a gay man, but I like to forget about that.

"It means," she says, putting our book down and resting her head on my hip, "that women smell like the ocean."

I wonder how a gay man would know this, but I cannot wonder for very long because Cecile is burrowing her nose between my thighs.

"You smell like the Atlantic," she says. "At night."

"Don't you want to find out what happens next?" I tease. I mean in the book, but Cecile answers, "This does," while her tongue separates myself from myself.

Cecile finds my wettest spot and laps it with her tongue. Then she turns, leans, and half-straddles me for a deep, long kiss. Her mouth tastes like a midnight sea. I kiss her back, clasping for a hold on the hair at the base of her skull.

"Good night, honey," she says. "I love you."

"I love you, too," I whisper.

Cecile unstraddles me and turns off the light. She tangles her limbs around mine as if we are two trees sharing the same taproot.

One of the most sensual things Cecile and I do between our sheets, as the stars of the summer sky witness through our windows, is sleep together. The darkness calls us into each other. We sleep touching, always touching—our ankles wrapped, or my hand on her breast, or her arm on my thigh, or my hair trapped under her head. We sleep, talking, saying, "I love you, honey," or, "Are you O.K.?" or, "Hold me," or,

"I'm having a bad dream."

Cecile dreams of rattlesnakes, poised and ready to strike.

I dream of Dulcie, screaming that I was a dolt not to see she loved me.

Cecile and I shake in our nightmares, waking each other. We find words for our fears and use these words to find the magic of sleep again.

Sometimes it is a barking dog that wakes us. Sometimes it is Bob the cat who jumps on my head. Sometimes Colby yells from his bedroom. Sometimes we wake up with the sun, holding hands like a pair of school girls who have just returned from a field trip to the universe.

I rarely slept with women before I met Cecile. I fucked them, went to bed with them, had sex with them, rolled with them, laughed with them, teased, licked, and kissed them. I was manic in those preciously dark hours between the closing of bars and dawn. But sleep was too safe to be shared. I thought danger was the only aphrodisiac, sex the only shelter.

Love, of course, was a trap. Not dangerous, but deadly. Not intoxicating, but addictive. If I was in bed with a woman silly enough to mutter the word *love*, I would be back on the street as soon as escape was possible. I would walk home in the night air, which would feel crisp, no matter how hot; which would feel comforting, no matter how cold.

"I love you," Cecile says, rolling out of bed.

"Mmm," I say, still hugging our sleep. I hear the water running and the cabinet doors open and close. The toilet flushes. Cecile returns to bed with two hot cups of coffee spiked generously with half-and-half.

The mornings are our favorite time to make love. I am often late for work, but since I have been promoted to supervisor at the Department of Motor Vehicles, this matters less than it once did. Today, however, is Saturday, as Cecile reminds me, her voice luxurious with the uniquely extra syllable of it.

I rest my cheek against the hard flat bone between her breasts. It smells like the white pulp of an orange rind, the pericarp, slightly acidic and slightly sweet. I used to slide that flesh between my teeth as a child. "Don't eat that," my mother would scold. But I always did.

Cecile's breasts are soft and shaped like navel oranges. I lick her stiffening nipples with my coffee-coated tongue. I kiss her eyebrows, her jawbone and cheekbones, her mouth. She arches her back, and my fingers slide across her stomach and then under her. I settle one hand into the mold of her back. With my other hand I stroke her and tell her I love her and how sweet she is and I love her and how wet she is and I love her. Cecile speaks a language of words with vowels only or with consonants only. I speak to her in stuttering English. I say, "More" or "Deeper" or "Let me." I say, "Come again for me," and she does.

The air is salty with sweat between us. Cecile is thirsty. I go to refill our coffee cups. Cecile is cold. I cover her with a damp pink sheet. I pick up the detective novel, thinking to read the next chapter aloud to Cecile. I do not even have a chance to find our place from last night when Cecile slips her leg under me. She holds one hand lightly on my wrist and the other on my face. I am still wet and open from touching her. When she enters me, I cannot be any more wet or open. Her face is close to mine. Our eyelashes touch each other's, blinking their own messages. I can hear her words, feel her breath, smell the salt on her neck.

Her eyes are where I go when I come. They are not limpid pools (as a child I wondered who would want a limp pool in her head), but more like the crystals that hang in our bedroom windows, refracting the morning sun. Her eyes are a hard but inviting place, with every color I have ever seen/heard/felt/tasted, and a few I have not. Sometimes, as I wander in her eyes, there are so many facets it seems like there must be a mirror hidden somewhere. There is not.

When I return to the bed from her eyes and my knees stop shaking I hear a voice that is not Cecile.

"My heart is beating."

I slowly move my hand to my chest. My heart is, in fact, beating. It has not flown from between my breasts into Cecile's eyes. I hear the voice again. It is impatient and childlike. I look at Cecile. Her mouth is closed but smiling. Her eyebrows arched.

"That's good, Colby," Cecile says, "your heart is supposed to beat."

"I'm Eric Bobcat today," Colby says, "and my heart is beating."

I focus on Colby standing near the bed. I did not even know he was awake, and he has already changed his name and brought it into the bedroom with his beating heart.

"Not long," Cecile answers, before I can ask her how long Colby has been witnessing my travels into her eyes.

"I want to sleep," I tell Colby.

I close my eyes. Cecile rearranges the sheets, including fitting the fitted sheet back onto the mattress corner. Her hand strokes my wet thigh. I open my eyes.

"I have an idea," Colby announces.

Then he is gone from the bedroom. I am ready to go back into Cecile's eyes. My tongue aches for a taste of Cecile.

Cecile and I are kissing. Colby is climbing into the bed. He has several books, one of which is sharp against my breast. He is smiling and smiling. One of the most passionate practices Cecile and I enact on our queen-size, with our child looking from face to face, is to alter the words in the Read-Aloud Series.

Learning To Read

I know it is cold because Cecile returns to bed after her shower with her socks on. She burrows under the quilt, twisting her ankles around mine. I can hear Colby in his own room singing out the alphabet. When I get up to make the coffee, I light the candles on the windowsills, as if this will keep us warmer.

"The coffee's already on," Cecile says. "Close the windows."

"It's only September," I answer.

"It's cold."

"We live in Florida," I remind her.

"*North* Florida," she reminds me. "We're not in Miami anymore."

I miss the smell of hibiscus. It is not yet autumn, and already the mornings are more chilled than February used to be. I think Cecile looks cute in socks, but I hate to wear them myself; socks make me feel like a child.

"You're not going to turn on the heat," she accuses.

"It will warm up."

"You're just like my mother," Cecile says. "You would rather freeze your ass off than use a little electricity."

"It isn't the electricity," I tell her, but I don't know what it is.

After spreading out a pair of Osh-Kosh overalls, a blue-and-white-striped shirt, some white socks, and Snoopy underwear for Colby, I lavish myself with a hot shower, grateful that Cecile has left me some steaming water. I imagine what I will wear to work, deciding on a purple pullover and lavender pants. Toweling my hair, I see Cecile walk into the kitchen wearing the purple pullover and lavender pants, as if she read my mind.

Colby is still singing the alphabet and he still has his pajamas on. The clothes, however, are on the floor.

"Get dressed!" I yell.

"What does this say?" Colby asks, pointing at the letters on his pajamas. Last year he was intrigued by the three wolflike dogs silkscreened on the pajama top. Now, he wants to learn to read.

"Chinook," I say.

"And what does this say?" Colby asks Cecile, as she brings me a cup of coffee.

"Team Sled Dogs," she reads.

"Look, a S, a S." Colby is excited.

"Yes. S starts the word *sled*. S-L-E-D," Cecile says patiently, as I am trying to wrestle Colby out of his pajamas, worrying that they are the warmest pair that he has, and he is wearing them in September.

"What's a sled?" asks the almost-five-year old who has never seen snow.

Cecile, who has also never seen snow, explains dogsledding to Colby. Although Cecile's childhood was in the subtropics, she spent most of it reading *National Geographic* magazines.

"Hurry up and get ready for primary." I change the subject. "If you are old enough to be in primary, you are old enough to get dressed yourself."

My suggestion has no effect on Colby, who is tracing the word *Chinook* with his finger. After two weeks in the primary section of the Co-op Free School, the word *primary* has lost its magic. After months of pleading and cajoling, Colby finally made his way across the fence into primary. Now, it all seems blasé. It depresses me to see one of the cruelest traps of life—that anticipation often leads to disappointment—already ingrained in a four-year old.

Cecile and I are also less than thrilled with primary, although in our case we did not have too many expectations. The school is the most "alternative" in this town with an alternative community consisting of people who usually live at one of the three land co-ops, shop (at least for cheeses) at the food co-op, take classes in weaving or computers at the University Without Walls Co-op Learning Center, and send their children until the age of eight to the Co-op Free School. While the scant women's community is often subsumed into the alternative community, when it comes to the Co-op Free School, it sometimes seems as if the word *co-operative* is not broad enough to include Cecile and me.

It also seems that co-operative excludes lots of other people. While the facade of the school is interracial—the walls are covered with magazine cutouts of mixed-race children who are attractive to the Anglo eye as well as being politically correct—the children who actually attend the school are as uniformly light-skinned as Colby. There is one child with a birthmark the size of a quarter on her cheek.

On the way to the school, Colby finally dressed, Cecile and I talk for the hundredth time about sending Colby to public school as soon as he is old enough. For now, it seems as if it is either the Co-op Free School or the Christian Academy.

But sometimes when Cecile and I walk into the co-op school with Colby between us, I think mornings facing the fundamentalists might be easier. It is not difficult to read the faces of the adults. *Surely, it only takes one of them to hold the boy's hand, keep him from dropping his lunchbox containing Oreo cookies although they have been told we disapprove of sugar, to sign him in.* With one of us, the teacher and her aides (all of them women, all of them married, most for the second time) can pretend we are not who we are. They can pretend that somewhere there is a happy husband rushing off at this very moment to committee work at the food co-op, or a responsible job at the university with walls, or at least to yet another episode of acceptably heterosexual infidelity. So, Cecile and I always walk in together.

This morning when we walk in we learn that September is Family

Month at primary. I do not notice the bulletin board at first because I am noticing how nice those lavender pants hug Cecile's thighs. Cecile elbows me, pointing.

WHAT IS A FAMILY? the block letters on the bulletin board ask. Underneath, the block letters respond: FATHER, MOTHER, SISTERS AND BROTHERS, YOU. To the side are three magazine cutouts: a white man and woman with a blond boychild and a blonde girlchild and a baby; a black woman and man with a brown-eyed, black-skinned boychild and a brown-eyed, black-skinned girlchild and a dark brown-skinned baby; and an Asian woman in a kimono with an Asian man in a business suit and an Asian-looking baby. The lines drawn around each of the pictures seem so thickly uncrossable that it makes me wonder how all those interracial children on the other walls got there.

I mean to comment on this to Cecile, but when I look at her I can see a storm gaining strength under her eyebrows. Cecile has the same sort of torrential temper as my mother. While Cecile spent her childhood looking at magazines, I spent mine reading the skies of my mother's eyes. As soon as I spot that certain cloud around the iris, I try to redirect the storm. This morning, with Cecile, I pull her out of the room, banging my knee on one of those two-foot-high tables.

I barely get the car door closed before the downpour.

"I have had it," Cecile screams. "Men. Men. Men. These stupid jerks and their fucking fathers."

"Cecile," I say.

"I'm tired of it. We pay all this money to send Colby to an alternative school and they shove that shit down his throat. Every family does *not* have a father."

"I know that, Cecile."

"Well, apparently those fools don't."

"I'll speak to someone." I am hoping that Cecile does not take me seriously. I am hoping Cecile knows that I am saying this to mollify her. I would be content to let it slide, perhaps light a pink candle. And then change schools.

"Good. Go talk to the director," Cecile says, taking me seriously.

Like any other two people who have known each other longer than five seconds, Cecile and I assign ourselves and each other roles. It would be easier, I sometimes think, if Cecile and I had more rigid roles—like breadwinner/homemaker or even butch/femme. Our life, however, has never been capable of being split into even such complicated dualities. Instead, I—the woman who won't close the windows no matter how cold it is because the calendar on the wall reads September—am being cast as the logical one of the co-mothers.

I open the door to the car. I try to remember the director's name, but I can only think of radio jingles for sugar-free candy. I clear my throat to make room for my "I-know-you-really-did-not-mean-to-be-an-insensitive-shit-but-your-homophobia-is-showing" tone of voice. Surely, I tell myself, it cannot be that difficult to talk to the director of an alternative kindergarten. After all, I am employed by the State of Florida in a responsible supervisory position—although I am dressed a little funkily and wish I had on those lavender pants. I decide upon the administrator-to-administrator approach.

But before I am inside the tiny office, I am being nagged about the garage sale to benefit the school. The director, whose name I still cannot recall, is reminding me that I have not yet donated any items and insisting that I must have something suitable.

"I'll look," I promise, not stopping to take a breath. "But what I really need to talk with you about is family month at primary. I'm a little troubled about the theme, especially the father thing. Not all children have fathers, you know."

Silence.

"Oh, I know that," she finally says. "It isn't meant to be offensive. And I really thank you for saying something. Parental involvement is what this school is all about. I'm so glad you spoke up. Parents sometimes think I can read their minds, but I can't."

I do not mention that there was never a need to read my mind. All she had to do was read any one of the seemingly hundreds of forms Cecile and I had to fill out to enroll Colby, forms with questions about pets, favorite colors, and maybe even the pets' favorite colors.

"Well," I finally say—

"Like I said," she says, "I'm really glad you shared your thoughts."

It is at times like this that I see the fury of Cecile and my mother as the logical response. I would like to rip the artfully knotted bandana from around the creamy neck of the director.

Instead, I am true to my role. My character resembles Antarctica more than a tropical hurricane. "What are you going to do about it?"

"I can take it up at the next Teachers' Planning Day."

"And when is that?"

"October 9th," she says.

"How convenient." I stalk out to Cecile.

I tell her about my conversation with the director. To Cecile's credit, she lets me finish before her curses fog up the windows. To my relief, she focuses her fury on the school's director.

After Cecile drops me off in front of my office building, I spend my time trying to sort out my politics, my responsibilities to Colby, and the Monday morning reports. I would like to put my personal life on hold, but the phone lines keep ringing with that distinct sound of a personal call. This one is long distance.

"It's Amber," the voice says. The buzz on the line tells me she is on the SUN-COM line, strictly for state business, but if she is still a traffic cop in Ft. Lauderdale, I suppose she could think of a thousand excuses to call me at the Division of Motor Vehicles.

"Long time no see," I say, though I suppose I am not seeing her now. I feel cynical. She must want something.

"I just wanted to tell you," she tells me, "that it's all coming true."

"What?"

"You know that reading you did for me before you left Miami? Well, it's all coming true."

I am trying to remember reading Amber's tarot cards. I remember February, the smell of hibiscus under the open window, Amber sitting on the floor of that raunchy apartment Cecile and I had in the Grove. Amber was in a tizzy about a dyke she fell in love with as she was ticketing her for double parking on Biscayne Boulevard.

"Everything is wonderful," Amber continues. "Logan and I are having a ceremony at Sea World. We want you and Cecile to come. Bring the kid, she might like it. And really, I want to talk with you about having a kid."

I am barely off the phone with Amber when my private line rings with its Cecile ring.

She can't meet me for lunch today. She's got the car. She's picked up Colby. She's home trying to figure out how to work the heat. She's going to make a list of our options. She'll pick me up at five.

"Four," I tell her. "I'll leave early."

She tells me that she loves me, that she'll be there at four, that she loves me, that we'll have soup or something warm for supper.

After a dinner of cheese soup and toasted-cheese sandwiches, Cecile produces her list. It includes suing the school, bombing the school, home-schooling Colby, starting a lesbian school, and moving to Cuba.

"My Spanish is shit. Besides, don't they lock up queers there?" I respond only to the last option.

"You could work on your Spanish. Besides, wouldn't it be neat to have Colby learn to read in Spanish? *Mira perro*," she says, ignoring my objection.

"The lesbian school is an interesting idea," I answer.

"Great, until you think of who else would be involved," she says, axing her own idea. "Can you imagine a school with Prissy-the-Nazi's kids?"

"Don't use the word *Nazi* so lightly."

"I'm not. What would you call her? Born in Paraguay after World War II, her father a German scientist."

"People aren't responsible for their fathers," I argue.

"Maybe not. But she sends her eleven-year-old son off to a military school in South Carolina because he was 'acting like a sissy'. She campaigns for Republicans. She may sleep with women, but she ain't a lesbian in my book."

"There are other people," I say, hoping Cecile does not ask me to name names.

"Whatever." Cecile smiles. "I think we should teach him to read at home."

"We already are."

Colby can pick out words like *and, the, moon,* and *ocean* from his favorite books. He has memorized the stories like poems, of course, but we are teaching him to see letters as words, to say words as sounds, to hear sounds as meanings. He is anxious to learn, as if he can smell freedom.

When I was learning to read, it was that same smell of freedom that intensified my hunger. Sitting on my mother's lap, I learned the skills which would make it possible for me to have a life different from hers. It was in a book where I first found out about women who loved each other. I like to imagine I was reading those books at the same time Cecile was sprawled in a windowseat reading *National Geographic* articles about women with dogsled teams.

For Cecile and me, learning to read allowed our world to be different from our mothers'. But now that Cecile and I are mothers, I find myself not wanting Colby's world to be different from ours.

I want to protect Colby from the F-word: father. I want to censor all those books with their perfect Daddy and Mommy dyads. I want to forbid all the fairy tales and legends and myths full of insipid women who are either bad or beautiful, and boys who are either handsomely virtuous or stupidly ugly. Since he was born, Cecile has been reading to Colby and changing the words. Now we are teaching him to read. Soon, he is going to figure out that MOM cannot be spelled both M-O-M and D-A-D.

Our phone rings.

"Who is it?" Cecile asks.

"The school," I say, without moving. My ability to know who is on the phone without answering it used to spook Cecile. After all these years, she now merely thinks it is convenient.

"Should I answer it?" she asks.

"Go ahead."

The poor mother (it is never a darling daddy) unlucky enough to be on our branch of the phone tree soliciting items for the Co-op Free School garage sale finishes her spiel to Cecile.

"If we aren't good enough to be represented in family month, then I doubt our white elephants are good enough for the garage sale." Cecile slams down the phone.

"I hate the whole idea of families," I tell Cecile.

"We've had that discussion a thousand times," Cecile estimates.

In less than an hour, the phone rings again.

"It's the school," I say.

"Even *I* know that," Cecile says, picking up the receiver.

"We *did* tell you how upset we are." Cecile is telling the director.

"No, I don't expect you to read our minds. We told you this morning." Cecile is raising her voice.

"Another bulletin board sounds like a pretty token gesture." Cecile is pretending to be even-tempered.

"Well, we'll talk it over." Cecile hangs up.

"Talk what over?" I ask Cecile.

"Oh, that jerk thinks she can fix everything with a bulletin board filled with photographs from the kids' families. We should send a picture with him on Wednesday. The teacher will do a collage."

While Colby is in the bathtub, Cecile and I talk about victory and compromise, about consensus and politics, about when we were kids. About being different from other mothers because we are dykes, and being different from other dykes because we are mothers, and about being different from other dyke mothers because we are who we are and who we are means we are different even from each other.

After Cecile's anger has subsided and Colby is clean, she wants to compromise by sending an outrageous photograph of the three of us.

After Cecile's anger has subsided and Colby is clean, I want to pull Colby out of school for Family Month.

After Colby gets into his Chinook purple pajamas, despite my argument that it is turning warmer, Cecile reads him a book. He claps whenever he spots *and* or *the* or *ocean* or *moon*. Cecile is trying to teach him *tree*. He becomes confused between *the* and *tree*. He whines and cries.

"No one said learning to read was easy." Cecile almost scolds him. "Now, do you want to learn to read or don't you?" she asks.

I am half-hoping he says no, but Colby says he will try harder. Cecile tells him to count whether there is one *e* or two. Colby smiles, learning another secret.

When Cecile is finally finished with the book and Colby has sung himself to sleep with the alphabet, Cecile and I relax in our bedroom. I watch as she takes off those lavender pants, a golden splotch of soup stained into the thigh. I light a candle on the windowsill. A damp night breeze blows through the open windows.

We sit cross-legged on our pink quilt. We look at each other, two women with a child asleep in the next room. This is the universe we have made. We have ourselves and we have each other and we have long conversations, sometimes with words that sprint from our lips to the other's ears, and sometimes with words that travel between us without moving through either time or space.

When we get out the tarot cards we each ask the same question: what should we do about the Co-op Free School? We spread the cards and pick them and talk about them. We get the Tower and Five of Discs and Son of Cups and the Star.

We decide we need some more practical advice. In the same moment, we are striding toward the phone, each of us wondering whether it is too late to call our mothers.

Our Mothers
& Their Mothers

Our mothers were not dykes. If they had been, our lives would be very different, not to mention the lives of our mothers. The mothers of our mothers were not dykes either, if being a dyke means being an outrageously-out lover of women. If they had been, our mothers' lives would have been very different, and our lives would be different, too, not to mention the lives of our mothers' mothers.

Cecile and I are sitting on the bed in Cecile's redecorated adolescent basement bedroom. Before this was called the guest room and Cecile became a guest in her mother's house, she used to sit in this room's coolness and read ambiguously lesbian novels, looking for the sex scenes. But even before those novels, Cecile used to sprawl across her twin bed and read ambiguously lesbian letters, looking for the sex scenes. The novels Cecile reads have become thankfully less ambiguous; the letters remain so.

Cecile assumes a precise falsetto and reads aloud: *"Come, come, my love and leave your empty life behind you like a bad dream. Come to my bed and spread your chestnut tresses where they belong."*

"And what does your grandmother say to that?" I ask.

"Oh, probably something about the cabbage crop."

"Hey, true love has many expressions."

"I doubt that." Cecile smiles a sarcastic, sexy smile, one eyebrow arched crookedly.

"For someone who writes *I love you* at the bottom of a grocery list as if it were another vegetable, you've certainly gotten particular."

"This is different." Cecile is adamant, challenging almost.

I decide to let it drop. I guess we all have things that aren't really open to discussion. For Cecile, her grandmother and Rebecca are one of those things.

Whenever we go to Cecile's mother's house, Cecile sneaks the wooden box of letters from her mother's room. She has read those letters so many times she practically has them memorized, but she always wants to read them again. Late at night, in the guest room bed, Cecile opens the box as gently as the first time she opened me. I tense with teenage excitement—afraid to get caught, afraid something will crumble. After a while though, I get bored with the *Darling*, the *Dearest*, the *My Everything*.

"They probably weren't even lovers," I say. I've said this before. And Cecile has gotten angry before.

"You're crazy," Cecile announces.

"I'm not. Remember the book by that woman about how this was just the way women talked back then?"

"You read too much."

"Me?" I squeal. "At least I don't read letters that aren't addressed to me."

I put the thin sheet over my head and pretend to sleep, while Cecile fingers the now-brittle ecru paper. She should pay so much attention to me, I pout. It always amazes me how excluded I can feel in the presence of a history we do not share.

Still, I start thinking about the letters, in spite of myself. It is rather interesting. Made more interesting by Cecile's mother's mother's disappearance. Did she leave the cabbage farm for Rebecca, the woman of the ecru letters? Or did she get on the train for some man? Or for herself? And did she regret leaving her daughters behind? Did she ever miss Cecile's mother, the woman in the upstairs bedroom who still hides a box of old letters in her dresser?

A small continent could be covered by the women who gave up their children for the women they loved. Some did it quietly. Some went deaf from the din of custody battles. Another small continent could be covered by the women who gave up the women they loved for their children. Most are silent. On every continent it seems like the choice is either/or: either lesbian or mother.

I'm exaggerating, I accuse myself. After all, I have both. Colby is upstairs, asleep, I hope. Although with his cousin Alex in the same room, there could be a major Monopoly marathon occurring despite the lights-out. Cecile is next to me, definitely not asleep, still reading those letters. I try to snuggle against her taut legs.

In the dressing room of a moderately priced department store at a medium-sized shopping mall the next afternoon, Cecile is trying on a pair of black cotton pants both her mother and I think will be too small for her. We wait patiently, her mother and I—after all, the pants are on sale—talking about fabrics, prices, and the tailored look. But then my tongue swells with the urge to ask her about her mother. I swallow. The silent hard swallow of my own mother, who taught me that questions are rude, that there are whole worlds better left unsaid, that there are words which, once spoken, swallow everything else.

Cecile returns without the pants. "A little tight," she says. Cecile's mother and I exchange confirming smiles.

Only once in all those shopping trips, all those long twilights of iced teas on the porch, all those car drives to relatives or hospitals or restaurants, do I ever hear Cecile's mother mention her mother. "My mother is dead," she says, simply.

Only once in all those long years of living crowded as Siamese twins did I ever hear my own mother say a word against her mother. "I wish she was dead," my mother said. Otherwise my mother said nothing. She swallowed a lot. My mother swallowed even harder when her mother began her long and jagged trip toward death.

My mother's mother was a sexy, cigarette-smoking woman who left life in an Appalachian mining town for life in a Brooklyn cigar-rolling factory. While Cecile's mother was waiting to marry off the cabbage farm, my mother's mother was bobbing her hair, buying Red Passion lipstick, and learning to drink gin. My mother's mother is a woman I might have resembled—or might have loved—had I been a baby dyke during the early days of World War II instead of the last bombings of the Vietnam War. I should name her prefeminist, claim her as a part of my class consciousness, consider her dyke potential, but my politics slam into the wall of my family.

She dumped my mother—her illegitimate, crying daughter—back at the coal fields with a distant cousin and then went on with her life as if my mother had never happened. Before Colby, I thought a mother's love was inevitable, its absence an aberration. Now I see it for the accomplishment it is. And like any accomplishment, it has a price: sometimes astronomical, sometimes so subtle that the tag is invisible. But marked or not, there is a price.

Part of the price my mother paid was the chance to reclaim her own mother. Abandoned long before, my mother nevertheless came to her mother's sickbed. If there is anything stronger than mother-love, it is daughter-love. My mother bent over her mother like a crescent moon bends over a star, nursing her mother like her mother had never nursed her. My mother's mother recuperated. My mother got pregnant. My mother's mother got illogical with fury: she threw her best dishes at her daughter, calling her a lesbian whore.

We are at a shopping mall when my mother tells Cecile this story. There is something about mothers and shopping, I think. But what I want is my mother to swallow, not to talk. I don't want Cecile to hear this story from my mother. I like my own version better. My mother's is too raw. I try to get my mother to try on a pair on pants, on sale.

"You should be glad I never talked to you like that," my mother says to me, for Cecile's benefit. "That I never accused you of being a lesbian or anything."

As if she could have changed the course of my history with a little discouragement.

As if she hadn't ever accused.

Now is not the time to bring up my mother's amnesia or her ineffectiveness. Not Jadine, who my mother saw walking down Eighth Street, her fingers entwined with mine. Not any of the girls I always seemed to find who wanted to practice kissing with our eyes closed as if we were eighteen instead of twelve, nine, eight. Not my mother's, "God damn it to hell. Stop acting as if you're queer or something." That time, my mother was cutting up onions into crescents at the clogged sink that would never get fixed. One doesn't complain when one is behind in the rent. My mother never complained. Except to me.

"And even if you're going to do that crazy lezzy shit, at least stick to your own kind." I guessed my mother was upset that Jadine's mother was from China. I swallowed hard, feeling a permission as vague as the rings around the moon I could see on a summer night. Women were my own kind, I thought then, but didn't say. Never really said.

Never really said anything that I thought might upset my mother. I swallowed. A lot. Just like I'm swallowing now. "Try on these pants," I plead with my mother. "They'd look nice on you."

"I'll need something black," my mother says, "for the funeral."

My mother's mother is dying, infested with cancer.

And Cecile's mother is also dying, from the same disease.

These days, Cecile and I seem to drag Colby from relative to relative, from hospital to hospital. Dying is very time consuming. We are busy as daughters. I'm exceeding my annual leave from the state. And I'm not even sure that my mother's mother and Cecile's mother fit into the civil service bereavement categories.

Cecile and I are spending another weekend at her mother's house. Only this time, Cecile doesn't have to sneak the letters from her mother's bedroom because her mother isn't here. Cecile and I sit on the porch, watching Colby and his cousin Alex play hide-and-seek. Alex' mother sits beside her younger sister, Cecile, trying to act as if their mother is not in the hospital. Cecile joins the hide-and-seekers. Cecile's sister Karen tries to entertain me with a repeat performance of the only story she ever tells me: the lesbian accusation screamed by Cecile's mother.

Only the accusation wasn't aimed at Cecile, which is apparently what makes this story worth telling for Karen. "No, not at our sweet baby, Cecile," Karen says, "but at me. Can you believe it?" she asks, not waiting for me to answer that of course I'd believe it. "All because of Cherry, the piano teacher. I mean, she was awfully nice, but really.

"What ticked Mother off," Karen continues, "was when Cherry came to the house to tell Mother I was a sensitive soul stuck in a house of people who didn't understand me. And that I needed extra attention. Mother hit the roof. Mother told her she didn't need to hear about her daughter from any piano teacher. And that her daughter didn't need attention from any l-l-l-l-esbian trying to corrupt her."

Karen always emphasizes the stutter of the word *lesbian*. I think it is her favorite part.

I look out toward the trees, trying to spot Cecile in the darkening yard. I see Karen's third husband fumbling in the darkness near the garage. I see Colby and Alex giggling on home base. I see Cecile striding toward the porch. "It's getting late," she says.

Later, in the basement guest room, Cecile spreads the letters across the bed. I try to distract her, although I should be grateful that she is thinking about anything other than her mother in the hospital.

"Karen told me the lesbian story," I tell Cecile.

"Karen's ridiculous," Cecile says.

"Are you sure you don't remember your mother ever calling Karen a lesbian?" I ask Cecile.

"Of course not," Cecile says. "Mother would never do that. She was always supportive of me."

"But was she supportive of Karen?" I ask, laughing. Cecile and I tried to match Karen with a nice woman in between her marriages, agreeing she'd be happier as a dyke. It didn't work, but we still think that it should have.

And was she supportive of her mother? I don't ask. Her own mother, who may or may not have been a lesbian, even if she wasn't a dyke. Her own mother, who received letters that read like love.

I don't ask Cecile because Cecile can't answer. Or the only answer that Cecile can give is that her mother was supportive, even if her mother wasn't. If Cecile gave a different answer, she wouldn't be supportive of her own mother. And being supportive is supposed to define mothers and daughters. It is even more important than shopping.

But whether or not it makes Cecile's mother supportive of her own mother, or of her daughter Karen, I still like Karen's story. It lets me imagine the newly adolescent Cecile, sitting on the stairs, watching her mother's anger at Karen's piano teacher. I imagine that Cecile heard in her mother's stuttered word an ambition. I imagine that as that linguadental-L ricocheted around the door frame, Cecile thought of me. Not the *me* I was then, running around the streets holding Jadine's hand, but the *me* I am now, reaching under the sheets for Cecile's hand. Cecile's hand that holds the letters that may be about the lesbian love of her grandmother.

If I had my grandmother's letters of lesbian love, perhaps I could forgive her for abandoning my mother. Perhaps I could cry at her dying. Instead, I clutch the hand of the child I love, even if he isn't a perfect daughter, and miss another day of work. Cecile and I have driven the interstate miles, with Colby singing in the back seat all the way, so that I can play the part of dutiful granddaughter. While my mother sits and stands and greets at the funeral parlor, being supportive of her dead mother and being supported by her dyke daughter-in-law, Cecile, I do what my mother cannot bear to do: I sift through my grandmother's apartment. I sort her belongings into three piles: garbage, Salvation Army, and things my mother might want. I find no wooden boxes, no letters. My mother's mother never learned to read or write.

A week and a thousand miles later I stand outside another funeral home, holding Colby's hand and missing more work. It is night and the moon waxes exorbitantly above us, like a street light. Cherry, Karen's long-ago piano teacher, walks from her car into the building. I watch her walk, as if it might confirm or refute Karen's story.

Cecile's mother and my mother's mother are both cremated, the cancer finally burned from their bodies. Back home, Cecile and I escape into our house. It is a womb we refuse to abandon. We hide under our own covers. Cecile doesn't want to eat or even cook. And now that she can look at those letters any time she wants to get them from our closet, she has lost interest in them. Even Colby is somber, his singing lost somewhere in his throat.

When I wake up in the middle of the night, assaulted by abstractions like *eternity*, I think of Cecile's mother and my mother's mother meeting in some far away place. What would they say, I wonder, each of these women who never took another woman's tongue with her own. At least not that Cecile and I know about.

For Love Or Money

Some days, work is just another cup of coffee without Cecile. Since I am now a supervisor, drinking coffee is included in my official state job description. It means I go to the bathroom frequently. And in my bathroom-sized office, I have a patchwork of white styrofoam cups, half-filled with cold coffee, beige from the dried milk, heavy from the solidified sugar. I have a few ceramic mugs on my desk: one with a pattern of ancient women's circles that Cecile ordered for me from some craft coven in Wisconsin; one that says The Best Man For The Job May Be A Woman that my former co-workers in Miami gave me when I left. In the mugs, which seem too heavy to carry all the way to the bathroom, I grow little fungus creatures. Today, I promise myself every morning, I will scrub these gifts, especially the one from Cecile.

The one from my former co-workers, too. I think their chosen slogan was rather inane, but it is the thought that counts. I miss these former co-workers—not as individuals, with problems and habits and boyfriends and second husbands, but as co-workers. I do not seem to have any co-workers now. I call the people I supervise my co-workers, but this is a bureaucratic lie. I evaluate them; they complain about me.

The figures in our paychecks demonstrate our lack of parity. They do not tell me tales of boyfriends and second husbands. I do not tell them amusing anecdotes about Cecile's latest grumpiness, waving my hands like she always does, calling forth the Cecile that lives inside me.

Instead, in my silence, I miss Cecile. I hate work because it takes me away from her. And from Colby. I hate the pull of the long days. I hate the pull of what are called benefits but are really necessities, like health insurance for Colby (if not for Cecile). I hate the pull of the state paycheck, the push of it.

The Division of Motor Vehicles is just another state agency in this state capital congealing with state agencies. Before I was pushed into the promotion of M-12 Supervisor, I worked as an M-10 Computer Clerk in the Miami satellite office. Most people think the town of Tallahassee is a satellite of the city of Miami, but in government many things are opposite of what most people think.

Generally, I do the same things I did in Miami. I input and retrieve information. This is computer slang for secretarial work. I also answer the phone, trouble-shoot, and handle citizen inquiries. As an M-12, I supervise other people's inputting, retrieving, phone answering, trouble-shooting, and handling of citizens. Once in a while I do something vaguely official. The other day I met with three attorneys, two women and a man, who work at the Attorney General's office. They explained to me that the state is being sued for discrimination. Not in hiring, but in issuing driver's licenses. The state is being accused of demanding more identification for Hispanic-looking applicants than from Anglo-looking ones. The attorneys say they do not think this is true. I say I would not be surprised if it is. The attorneys frown, as if they do not like my answer. The attorneys do not ask each other, *What can you expect from a dyke?*, at least not so that I can hear. The state is not an equal opportunity employer when it comes to the matter of sexual preference, but even the most conservative attorneys like to pretend they are above such petty prejudices.

I am telling Cecile about the attorneys while we are at the women's coffeehouse, where no coffee is served because caffeine has been recently added to the list of items that should be avoided as oppressive. Two women leaning against the wall seem to half-listen to our conversation, as Colby escapes from childcare and comes to grab Cecile's hand.

"Oh, the boy." The woman with the shorter hair says this, although if I had looked at the other woman first, I would have thought it impossible that any other living creature could have shorter hair than her.

"Yes," Cecile says, glaring.

"I couldn't help overhearing your conversation," the other woman says. "My name's Elzy. And this is Maura. My lover is an attorney working on the discrimination case."

"With the state?" I ask.

"No. For the plaintiffs." Elzy looks at me pityingly from her perspective of being in a relationship with a politically correct attorney. "How do you know about the case?" she asks.

"I work at the Division of Motor Vehicles."

"How awful. What could be more boring?" the woman who has been introduced as Maura says. I look over my shoulder for Cecile, but she has returned with Colby to the childcare corner where there are more interesting things to do than stand around sipping mineral water and talking about work.

"Don't be rude," Elzy scolds. "She probably loves her work."

"I don't do it for love. I do it for money." I wish Cecile were standing next to me.

"I can think of more interesting things to do for money," Maura winks, "especially being as cute as you are."

I am silent.

I am not one of those women who can say proudly: I am a former prostitute. I am not one of those women who can fly the subject of class like a flag: I grew up poor. I cannot readily admit I am damn glad to have a state job. Even a job where I have to answer the telephone, as if I were "just" a secretary, as if I did not go to college for a while on a National Merit Scholarship.

I try not to answer the phone at home unless I know it is Cecile. At work, I answer and answer the phone. It is rarely Cecile, at least not since Cecile started going back to school. Mostly it is a disembodied voice wanting to speak to someone's supervisor. I spend hours listening to my own officiousness. I become especially officious when there is a complaint about one of the "girls."

"No girls work here," I say.

"But I was just talking to one," the complainer protests.

"That's impossible," I answer. I pause. I explain: "That would be against state and federal labor laws."

"What?"

"Girls and boys cannot work. Education is compulsory until at least the age of sixteen."

"Let me speak with your supervisor," the voice demands.

"The Governor is out of town today. May I take a message?"

At this point the caller either disconnects or becomes conciliatory. There is no way to forecast the choice, although I often give myself odds. Fifty-fifty is the best bet.

The odds are usually about ten-to-one that my supervisor, the Honorable Governor of Florida, is out of town, although I can't say that I keep up with his schedule. My more immediate supervisor is a lot like the governor: they share the same first name, the same gender, the same vaguely criminal squint around the eyes, and they both travel around the state attending meetings with no practical purpose. The odds are only about two-to-one that my immediate supervisor is out of town on any given work day.

When my immediate supervisor, Bob, is in town, he never fails to ask me to go out to lunch. I always refuse. Lunch, I think, is dangerous because it is so innocuous. It is supposed to be casual and merely convenient. I am neither a casual nor convenient person. The Governor never invites me to lunch. I suppose he does not dine with queers.

Usually, I sit in my office, drink coffee, and eat the sandwich and fruit Cecile packed for me. I have a pink plastic bag, the color of our bedroom walls, that I use every day. Colby has a Snoopy lunch box that he brings to primary. I have sliced olives on my cream cheese sandwich; Colby does not. I think about Colby when I eat my lunch. I think about Cecile.

I think about loving Cecile. I think about loving her not too much, or too long, but somehow maybe it is too deep. Loving Cecile feels like some semiclear liquid has seeped into my bones, leaving my hardest parts as much in shreds as the time I tried to clean the coffee stains from Cecile's favorite pair of white pants by soaking them overnight in a pan of undiluted Clorox.

Sometimes Bob, not the Governor Bob but the Division of Motor Vehicles Bob, comes into my office and talks to me while I am eating. Sometimes he talks about his first wife and his second divorce until his words swell my bathroom-sized office. Perhaps because I hate to munch grapes in front of people, I find myself talking back. I tell Bob trivialities about Cecile, about Colby. If he finds it odd that my life is unlike his, it does not show beneath his liberal beard.

I like our conversations best when we talk not about us, but about the nature of things. We talk the way Cecile and I used to talk before she went back to school. Today, with his knees crossed and cramped on the other side of my desk, Bob is waxing on the nature of romantic love. He is thinking of going back to his first wife.

"Maybe there is that perfect person out there for each of us," he says.

"Maybe," I agree. I think of Cecile.

"But what happens if we do not recognize her when we see her?" he wonders.

"You did," I reassure. "But it is often easy to forget what you remembered."

"Remembered?" he asks.

"Plato's *Symposium*," I answer. We have discussed this all before, even the part where Plato has the characters talking about true love; even the part where we are all really two people but get tragically separated and spend our lives looking for our other halves; even the part where homosexuality is explained.

"Ah, yes," he strokes his beard. He poses professorially. Despite the fact that we are in my office, I feel like a captured co-ed. I feel like that college impostor, the girl who whored her way into the hallowed halls of academia. I feel sick.

"Excuse me," I say, getting tangled in his legs as I escape down the hall and into the office-sized women's room.

Startled, or perhaps distracted with more enticing noon plans, Bob disappears from my lunch ritual. I am unpleasantly surprised to notice that I notice his absence. I do not finish my cream cheese sandwich but pick out the sliced olives and eat them. I begin to wonder what it would be like to go to bed with Bob, to go to bed with a man not for money. Cecile has done this. She has never told me about it, but she has told me about being married. Married only for a few months and to a supposedly gay man. But married is married. Married is fucked.

To stop my own stupid thoughts, I take a slug of cold coffee and walk out of my office. The other workers in the office silence themselves when they see me. It is Friday, and the office talk has been of weekend plans and lottery fantasies. Now there is only the barking of computer keyboards, the futuristic blur of incoming phone calls, the modulated tones used for citizens. I bring another styrofoam cup of coffee back to my cubicle. Sounds rush behind me, as if I were walking away from the ocean suddenly alive with a storm.

I sip more coffee.

My stomach is killing me, but still I sip more coffee.

I look over a monthly report. Last month's.

I decide I should clean my ceramic cups but do not want to part the sea of my co-workers to get to the bathroom's running water.

When my phone rings with its special Cecile ring, I jump on it, but I let it ring another time before answering it.

It is not Cecile. It is Maura.

"Cecile gave me your number," she says.

Well, I think, at least I was close.

"I need to see you. I've got an emergency."

"Come to the office," I say. I do not like Maura, remembering her from the women's coffeehouse. The smugness of women like Maura confounds me. Despite, or perhaps because of, those philosophy courses I took in college, I often engage in the fallacy of duality. There are two kinds of people in the world, I say. There are those who have money and those who do not. Or there are those who drink coffee and those who will not. Or there are those who have been married and those who have not.

Or there are those who stood with their sandals slipping off the curb, listening to the smooth sound of a late-model car as it slows and its power window glides down, peering inside to see what could be seen about danger and risk and price, and then answering the question, "How much?"

And there are those who have not. Never had to.

Like Maura.

But she's a dyke, and dyke is help offered whenever it is needed.

Maura is a tarot card reader. So am I, of course, but Maura dresses the part. She jangles into the office with her cotton pants that gather at the ankle and colored strings tied around her extremeties and loops of silver through her ears and nose. She looks like a white and privileged child dressed up as a gypsy for Hallowe'en. My co-workers stare.

Maura delivers her problem in circles, concentric and dramatic. It sounds for a while as if she had been kidnapped by a car salesman from Dodge Country; then as if she had burned her to-be-traded-car during the candle and incense farewell ritual. I listen, wondering if this is too insignificant to confide to her friend's lover, the politically correct attorney mentioned at the coffeehouse. I listen, assuming that she will explain the problem sooner or later.

She does. The title application lists her as the lien holder and Southeast Bank as the owner. She shows me a crumpled piece of paper. She cries, as if the whole universe has turned vice versa.

"Don't worry, Maura," I say, sounding like someone's mother, remembering that I am someone's mother, "the information was just input incorrectly. It's easy to fix."

I take her to a terminal, call up the file, switch Block A and Block B, print a revised title application. It takes about two minutes.

"I hate computers," she says. If Colby was standing there clutching that piece of paper, I would say, *You're welcome*, in that sarcastic tone that makes him quickly say, *Thank you*, acknowledging his forgotten manners. As a mother, it's my duty to instill consideration. My obligation to the family of dykes does not extend that far.

"I think I'll go put a hex on that place. Stupid salesman. Screwing up the title application like that." Now that there is no reason to be angry, Maura is angry.

"What about ethics?" I am suddenly hungry for an abstract conversation about the nature of things.

"Fuck ethics," Maura says.

"Besides," I add, "what could be a worse curse than being a used car salesman?"

I think this is funny, but I do not have a chance to laugh because Maura laughs for me as she answers, "Being a supervisor at the Department of Motor Vehicles."

Division. It is the *Division* of Motor Vehicles. But I do not correct her as she walks down the hall. My co-workers smirk slightly, pretending to be fascinated with their terminals.

I think I'll have another cup of coffee.

I think I'll go and pick up Colby early. I think I'll go home and try to talk with Cecile.

Interlude

I'm spitting out toothpaste into the bathroom sink when I experience an epiphany. Not one of those once-in-a-lifetime epiphanies that changes one's life. Not even one of those once-a-year religious epiphanies that come on January 6. But a daily, ordinary epiphany. An epiphany that doesn't embarrass me as I brush my teeth. A comfortable epiphany.

I'm not surprised to find this epiphany in the bathroom with me. For hours it has been hinting itself. When I looked at my work desk at the end of the day, it was clean: phone calls returned, memos circulated. I could smell the sweet progress of work, sweet even if the work was government administration. When I got to the roller-skating rink to pick up Colby, I saw how two older boys smashed their skates into his. He kept going, around and around the rink, intent on his own wheels. I wanted to run across the rink and kiss him, but I stood still until he saw me. Then I waved back.

When Colby and I got home, Cecile was humming a song I don't mind, making dinner. The noodles were al dente, the nuts were sweet, the red peppers were crunchy, and the mushrooms were large. Colby added a basil leaf to each plate, picked from the plant that seemed to be recovering from either under- or overwatering. Cecile talked about a new art show while we ate. She kissed my neck afterward and even did the dishes without complaint.

Hoping that the pine nuts are out of my gums (even if I didn't floss), I know I can bring this epiphany out of the bathroom and into the bedroom. In bed with Cecile, she and I will make love. Or we will not. It doesn't matter. My breath is minty and it will be minty tomorrow night. If we don't make love, there is tomorrow.

In the bathroom, I realize I am happy, that I want nothing different, not to be anywhere different. I am so happy and content I can deflect the anxiety about being happy and content. I can deny my heritage. Almost. Like all girls of my culture, class, and climate, I was raised on tragedy. My mother's job at night did not prevent her from following what she called the stories and what others called soap operas or daytime dramas. I stayed home from school, sick with a cold, or well with the luxury of a snow day, watching my mother iron while she watched TV. I knew Lisa from "As The World Turns" and Vanessa from "Love of Life" better than I knew my neighbors. Neighbors got evicted; Lisa and Vanessa were eternal. Only their children grew up and moved away. Then they came back with their secrets and amnesias. The sons returned haunted by shady business deals. The daughters returned pregnant and not knowing who the father could be. The absent father was my favorite theme. I just loved all those parthenogenic pregnancies.

There was another theme, too: happiness is disallowed. Happiness is not natural. Happiness is illusory. Even for people with driveways, new cars, nice clothes, and gardens. Even for people who know only doctors and lawyers. Even for people who live in places called Oakwood. Happiness is fraudulent.

I knew that if there were two people kissing on the TV screen (perversely, it was always a man and a woman), it wasn't real. It wasn't real not because TV shows aren't real, but because their pretend happiness wasn't even real within their pretend world. It was always as if one of them, however passionate a kisser, had her (or his) fingers crossed behind her (or his) back. My mother knew who was a betrayer, and as she sprayed water on a blouse she was ironing, she would let me know by hissing out *bitch* or *bastard* as appropriate. If I hadn't been home from school lately, I'd ask for the details. She would tell me which of the two kissers was cheating on the other, or which one wanted the other only for the money, or which one really wanted to be kissing someone else.

But even if both kissers *thought* themselves happy, clutching each other instead of crossing their fingers, loyal viewers knew it wasn't true. One had amnesia. One was pregnant. Or the kissers' parents were arch enemies. Or the kissers were siblings, separated at birth. Whoever they were, as they kissed, the phone would ring with its bad-news ring.

One time the kissers were married. To each other. I was home all week from school with a winter flu and watched them kiss at break-fast on Monday. It was an ordinary kiss, in front of their ordinary children. The introduction of these ordinary characters did not seem par-ticularly promising. I noticed they ate bacon. On Tuesday they kissed their ordinary kiss at dinner. They talked about their ordinary children who were someplace else. I couldn't tell what they were eating. By Wed-nesday their plot hadn't thickened. They kissed and said they loved each other. On Thursday they got their longest segment: they're kiss-ing in bed, with their hair and the sheets disheveled so that us sophisti-cated viewers will realize they've been having sex. They say how happy they are. How they've never been happier. How much they love each other. After all these years. They marvel at themselves.

I watched them transfixed. Not because I'd never seen happiness like this before, even though I hadn't. But because even at nine, I was waiting for the ax to fall. I was waiting for the phone to ring. I didn't know their secret but knew there must be one.

The last segment on Friday was always a cliffhanger. This week the viewers get treated like passengers in a car. We hear the tires squeal, see the glass crash into our windowed screen. Then it is dark. We hear si-rens. We hear the telephone. "There's been an accident."

One of the happy kissers is dead.

Next week there will be operations and doctors and doubts, but I knew the kisser was dead. Dead from too much happiness. I knew this, even though I'd be back at school next week when one of the doctors made the final pronouncement. I'd be sitting at a desk torn between wanting to study and go to college and wanting to get up and walk out of that place and never come back.

When I got to college I took a course in the classics. Greek drama wasn't much different from the daytime variety. Instead of names like Lisa and Vanessa, the characters were called Clytemnestra and Oedipus, but the basic plot was the same. Humans are not meant to be happy. To be happy is to commit *hubris*, to piss-off the gods, to bring down their jealous wrath.

It took me three years to walk out of that college. Once I left I never went back.

I wanted happiness that wasn't innocence. I wanted romance that wasn't tragedy.

I found Cecile. But even tonight, in bed with her and my epiphany, there's still a large piece of me that is afraid to be happy. I kiss Cecile and whisper that I love her. I hide my epiphany under the sheets, telling it to be quiet.

Maybe if we're silent, those jealous gods won't notice.

If the phone rings, I won't answer it.

It could be someone calling to tell me Cecile is my sister, or it could be someone calling to tell me I'm a bitch for being happy while my mother still has to work all night. Or it could be someone to take Colby away. Or reveal my amnesia.

The phone doesn't ring, not even once, during the night. Or the next night. Or the next. . . .

California,
Or At Least
Somewhere West

Cecile woke up in California for the second time that morning. Her first California was a dreamy coast of moderation: slow sunshine, gentle waves, easy breezes. She fell back to the inland of sleep. Her last California was all sweat and nauseousness, as if her body were almost a thousand miles of rocky coastline, stretching to puke a blue streak into the humid glare of the Pacific.

Water, whether navigable or not, is always a good cure. Even water that turns tepid too fast. Even water that smells like a rusted Brillo pad.

She steps from the shower into February Florida. The bathroom hums from the tiny heater, plugged into the outlet at the base of the medicine chest. Without her glasses, without her new contacts, she can see the blooming camellias on the other side of the molded window. The flowers are a thick pink, looking more plastic than petal. Cecile likes the half-opened buds the best.

Her lover loves them all: the half-open, the fully open, the too-far open, the ones rotting on the wet ground. Her lover, who tends toward the garish. Her lover, who dumps coffee grounds on the roots of the camellias. Her lover, who bought the tiny heater. Her lover, who wants to move to California. Maybe.

I am her lover.

For the past few weeks, Cecile and I have been discussing what we call the relative merits of staying in this old farmhouse in Miccosukee, Florida, and leaving for some city-state like San Francisco. We vacillate wildly. I have always believed in running away as a solution, even if I had no where to run—especially then. But now I'm not running *from* anyone or anything, and that makes running hard. Besides, I love this old house that Cecile and I have scraped and painted, sanded and polished, rescreened and rewindowed. We've poured our love into this house as if we would live here forever, as if we owned it and it owned us.

But we don't own it and we won't live here forever—or even another month—and I've got to tell Cecile.

I've got to tell Cecile that while she was in the shower, Dick Hurbert, our semiliterate landlord who works at the country JOY-MART where we go to pay our rent ($220, cash only), drove up the dirt road to give us his news.

"Yes," he says, "old man Klemp sold the place, 112 acres and everything. Some developer. Never thought the old man would do it." Dick Hurbert is now out his rent collection commission, probably a good twenty-two dollars a month.

"Sorry that y'all will have to move. The closing's not till March 1. I hope you can find a place."

"Sure, it'll be easy," I lie.

"Now, if you need me to get some legal type letter, I can get someone to draw you up something official."

"That's not necessary," I smile.

Dick Hurbert smiles back, sticks his head back into his pickup, and drives back down the dirt road. I haven't even opened the gate the whole time. Not more than two minutes, but enough time to change my life.

If Cecile wasn't already in the bathroom, I'd go in there and vomit. Instead, I pace around the place, the walls we have painted pink and lavender, the floors we have sanded and shellacked. I am sitting on

Colby's bed, staring at the starred ceiling, when Cecile comes out of the bathroom, still dripping from her shower. She looks so sexy with a rose-colored towel half-wrapped around her.

"Was that Colby?"

"No," I say. Cecile is always nervous when Colby spends the night away from home, even when he is staying with his two best friends in the entire universe, Latisha and Stan, children of his favorite teacher at the Co-Op Free School.

"Who was it?" Cecile asks. We do not get many visitors.

I am looking away, still looking for a way not to tell Cecile, still looking for a way to rearrange the truth.

"Something's wrong. Tell me," Cecile insists.

"It was Dick Hurbert," I answer, not answering.

"That old bastard isn't going to fix the backyard, is he?" Cecile asks. Cecile and I have repaired doors and roofs and fences, but when it comes to a hole near the septic tank, we figured we had better let the "property manager" do something. I had told Dick Hurbert about it in August, and he'd been promising to come check every month. Cecile has put some boards over it, so the cat or the child doesn't fall in, but the boards keep sinking.

"He's not a bastard," I say, because I don't like the word. Colby, after all, is a bastard.

"O.K.," Cecile concedes. "Just tell me what's wrong."

"O.K." Silence.

"Just say it." Cecile waits, knowing me well enough and long enough to realize she can do nothing else. Still, it makes her impatient.

"They sold the place."

"Oh, shit." Cecile puts her hands on her hips.

"Maybe the sale won't go through," I say.

"And we're still in Kansas, Dorothy." Cecile is saying this with more sarcasm than she intends, or at least that's what I'm hoping. Once, when we were reading to Colby, we started talking about which children's character we would each like to be. Colby wanted to be Nimby the Cloud or Baby Cougar. I suggested Sleeping Beauty for Cecile because I love to watch her sleep, but Cecile said she had always wanted to be one of the Hardy Boys. I thought I might like to be Glinda, the Good Witch, but I couldn't remember whether she was East or West, so I said I'd be Dorothy.

Cecile laughed. "You could never be Dorothy. If you were Dorothy, Oz would never have happened. You would spend the whole adventure denying reality, saying 'Hey, Toto, I think we're still in Kansas.' You are just not Dorothy material."

"Am I really that bad?" I asked.

"Yes," Cecile said.

By the time I thought that I would have been a perfect Dorothy—after all, it was a dream and she really didn't leave Kansas, did she?—it was too late to say it. Cecile was reading to Colby again.

Cecile still brings up Dorothy as a code for my habits of denial. I am again thinking that Dorothy would have been better off denying the yellowness of the brick road since it was only her sidewalk looking jaundiced in the tornado. I walk to the door and look down the dirt road that is our private driveway. Suddenly, I am hoping that a tornado tears this land to shreds.

I've never known what to do with emotions that spiral like anger and rage. I've never learned how to cope with that bottomless whirlpool that makes me think of the vengeful furies who had to be suppressed in the Greek plays I studied in college. I overflow with hate: for the developer who bought this property; for the old man who sold the land; for all the nuclear families who will buy half-acre plots, fence and landscape them, and barbecue key steaks in their backyards.

But like any good student of Greek drama, more than the people, I hate the idea. I hate the idea that land is something to be bought and sold and owned. Not in one of the philosophy or classics courses, but probably in a required class in American Studies, I was forced to read James Fenimore Cooper. Another stupid white man, but at least he had one thought attributed to him which I found sufficiently interesting to write down and tape somewhere in the room I "rented" from my lover: *The air, the water and the ground are free gifts to man, and no one has the power to portion them out in parcels.*

I was not sophisticated enough then to de-gender the word *man,* just as I was not sophisticated enough to appreciate that the woman I called my lover was, in fact, my pimp. I was being portioned out in parcels, certainly not a free gift to any man. I suppose I felt some affinity with the air, water, and ground. I took the quote when I left her, stuffing it in the case from the camera my aunt had given me.

I am the angry land—bought and sold, sold, sold. I want to destroy and be destroyed. Living on in me is that college scholarship student, the one educated by someone else's grace who paid with her body for her books. And that kid with the fantasies, the one watching another landlord hand her mother another eviction notice. And that woman with the state supervisory position, the one who is allowing her lover and her child to be told where they must live their lives.

I am the kid who went to college and became a state worker. I am an angry woman. The world is a mirror reflecting my anger back at myself.

I am angry because I believed this land was somehow sacred and could not be bought or sold. I am angry because I acted as if I owned this place. I am angry because Cecile and I have poured our money and our love into this old house when it didn't belong to us and never would.

I am crying.

Cecile is holding me, stroking me, telling me it will be all right. Oh, Cecile. How we have loved here. This house is alive with our round loving.

We have loved in other places, too. In a one-windowed duplex, in a house with a washing machine in the bathroom closet, in a basement apartment. And we will love at the next place we move, and the next. But our love here is spacious; it has seeped into the structure and fertilized the land. Isolated in the country with no neighbors to shove or shape our love, it has expanded like a contented cloud in the sky-blue sky.

"Let's go to California," Cecile says. "Right now."

She smiles her impossible smile.

"We weren't thinking of going until summer," I say.

"Yes, but we can go now."

"February is a terrible time to leave Florida."

"It's almost March," Cecile argues.

"We don't have enough money."

"We'll never have enough," Cecile argues again.

"You are in the middle of your semester."

"I'll quit," offers Cecile.

"That would be stupid."

Cecile's eyebrows crunch together searching for a retort. She is silent.

"Really," I say, still hugging her tight. "Let's go get Colby."

"I dread telling him. He loves this place as much as we do." Now it is Cecile who seems like she is going to cry.

Explaining it to Colby is easier than either of us anticipated. At five, life is his endless adventure. He wiggles with enthusiasm.

"Are we moving to California?" he asks.

"No, not yet."

"Then where?"

"We don't know exactly, yet."

"About where?"

"Somewhere west, yes, somewhere west of where we live now."

"Have you decided that, Cecile?" I ask.

"No, but I figure just about every place for rent will be west, toward town. And that way," Cecile smiles, "we'll be closer to California."

"Is west left or right?" Colby displays his primary school knowledge.

"Neither. Or I guess it depends on which way you're facing. But it's the direction of the setting sun."

"Oh." Colby is satisfied. But only for a moment. "Where does the sun go after it sets?"

"California," I say, forestalling Cecile's explanation of orbits and rotations. The tilting axis of the earth makes me nervous.

Cecile opens her mouth as if to protest, but she only says evenly, "Let's go get the newspaper."

Unfurnished Houses for Rent is our column. *No pets, no children* are the phrases we cross out, reducing our possibilities by half.

"Isn't that against the law?" I ask Cecile.

"The *no pets* or the *no children*?" she asks back.

Married couple only knocks out another possibility.

"Now, that has just got to be against the law," I tell Cecile.

"Does it matter?" Cecile asks.

It takes us five days to find a place that could be our home. Five days of circling want ads and streets, of consulting the map and dialing the phone and driving into a town where we do not necessarily want to live. There is nothing in the country; we are disappointed, but not surprised.

For five days we exercise and then surpass even our well-toned cynicism by comparing linguistic descriptions in the ads with physical realities. We discover that *nice* means barely livable; that *den* means unheated garage; that *deck* means two rotting two-by-fours in the backyard. What we are willing to pay for rent rises, and then rises again.

Colby, our good-luck charm, is thrilled with every place we visit. After we tell him that there is another place we want to look at, he starts looking forward to the next address. It is difficult to get depressed with him in the back seat.

But it is also difficult for me not to get depressed. Like every mother, I want the best for my child. Still, as we travel the streets inspecting rentals, I am saying that I will not tolerate my child (and my lover and myself) living in places a thousand times better than I lived in as a child. I would have given either my right or left arm, or so I thought then, to live in a house. Whether or not it was nice, or had a den that was a garage, or had a few boards in the backyard I always craved.

Finally, we find a place we could call home. It is too expensive, the carpeting is a thin vomit-green color, the bedrooms are tiny, but there are two of them. It is twenty miles west of Miccosukee; twenty miles into town. I tell Cecile that I want it.

What I really want is to stay where we are, to see the wisteria bloom and the redbud tree open, to act as if nothing has happened. If I were really the Dorothy-we're-still-in-Kansas that Cecile says I am, I would wait here until the sheriff came with those final papers which made throwing our stuff onto the dirt road quite legal. I would take the rifle we bought to shoot rattlesnakes and gun down this single personification of the whole system of private property. I could be a rural Eleanor Bumpers.

I don't have the guts. I am a runner. I would run to California right now if I could. I always go. Quietly. And quickly.

I cry winter-hot tears into Cecile's exhausted back as she sleeps. Cecile is probably tired, not from moving our stuff, but from being unusually cheerful and optimistic. I guess because Cecile can see that I'm as jagged as the scratch across my leg from the dresser as it swiveled against me in the narrow door, she's suppressing her sexy grumpiness. That's what love is all about: only one of us falling apart at a time.

At home I could always look at the pink walls, pinker in candlelight, and know Cecile loved me. Just seeing that shade of pink marketed as Scheherazade made me smell Cecile's sweat rolling down her forearm as she stretched for a corner with her paint roller. At home I could always gaze at the floors and find myself. Once covered with the grime of thousands of careless footprints, then stripped and sanded and sealed until the shine was like the contented safety of a framed mirror.

Home.

I am no longer home.

We go back home every day and every night looking for and not finding our cat. We last saw Bob walking down a dirt road that would soon be paved and named a developmentally trite name, like Bobcat. Something lost, never to be regained.

In our new house I bang against the unfamiliar shadows. I am a pale bridesmaid without a wedding, invisible against walls which taunt their whiteness, even at night. I am an uprooted tree floating across the moldy moss pile of the carpet. I am that helpless child, that streetwise student, that underpaid state employee.

I am the storm outside. I am rain, wind, cold. I am angry elements. I am a tornado. I am the furies.

I dream the old farmhouse burns down. I dream I shoot the developer. I dream the land swallows the neatly gridded development. I dream the camellias emit poisonous gases.

I dream I wake up in California, twice, Cecile waking up wet beside me.

Childress, Texas

Cecile is singing along with the Bonnie Raitt tape, something about needing a real man. Raitt sounds gutturally sincere, and after about twenty or so sing-a-longs, Cecile has lost her sarcastic falsetto and is singing like she means it. Only the way she lifts her eyebrows at inappropriate moments reminds me that she can't possibly mean it. She is Cecile and she doesn't need a man, real or otherwise. She is Cecile and she is a dyke.

Colby is singing along with the mixed voices of *Kid Songs 2*, something about a desperado in Colorado. The singers perform privately into Colby's twenty-two dollar tape recorder without rewind capacity but with earphones. Colby is as tuneless as Cecile, but since I can't hear the accompaniment, he sounds much worse. He also has a tendency to scream so that he can hear himself.

Every few minutes I yell, "Shut up!"

Colby takes off his earphones and says, "What?"

"Try to keep it down," I say. And he does try, or so it seems for a little while at least.

I am driving. Into the sunset, our car loaded trunk and top with belongings. The map is spread on Cecile's lap. The land spreads flat in front of me, flat on both sides of me. The only relief is the slight curve of distortion in the rearview mirror.

"What's that called when open spaces make you crazy?" I ask Cecile, interrupting her attempt to perfect her twang.

"I don't know. Maybe agoraphobia. Something like that."

We are in the middle of the country. The middle of nowhere and everywhere. Marking time by distance. Setting destinations with arbitrary rationality. Far enough from Dallas. Amarillo if we are set upon by a strange cloud of ambition. Childress as a place with a hotel. Also a museum chronicling the history of the Texas panhandle, or so Cecile had read aloud from our *AAA Tour Book*. Not a must-see starred attraction, but in a listed city nevertheless: pop. 5,500, alt. 1,877 ft.

It sounds exotic. I am excited to be a tourist in Texas, knowing that I am not supposed to be even remotely pleased. Tourista. Insult. Instead, I should consider myself a traveler, someone in the tradition of the great white hunters who colonized this continent, among others. I should avoid the Panhandle Museum with its ordinary items transformed into artifacts by the addition of fading index cards: *Wooden posts utilized by 19th C. Settlers*. I should instead range the panhandle itself with its ordinary items transformed into authenticity by my perceptive acumen. As if I could recognize authenticity in a place I'd never been; I could barely recognize it in places I'd lived for years and years.

And I should avoid being in this car with people who could be described as my family. I should, instead, be flagging down this car with my thumb, casually signaling that I'm available to accept a ride and offer adventure. There would be nothing furtive about me, nothing desperate about me, even though night was coming and I was here alone on Route 287 with only my rucksack. Maybe a guitar.

Like so many girls of my generation, I read Jack Kerouac, admired James Dean, sang "Truckin' " along with the Grateful Dead. I cross-dressed my daydreams, my dirty jeans sliding on my adolescent hips. Maybe a motorcycle. I wanted the same women the guys did. I guess that's why it took me longer than it should have to realize why the adventures of Jack and James and even Jerry Garcia weren't going to be mine. At times, I contemplated cross-dressing more seriously, more strategically.

"I wonder how many dykes came out here in covered wagons, masquerading as married couples," Cecile interrupts my road reverie. Right subject. Wrong century. Our thoughts are tangible to each other in the small space that is our car, but today we keep missing connections.

"Lots, I bet."

"Yeah, but we'll never know if even one did."

"We do know," I insist. "Think of us. We would have done it."

"You love me enough to go across a danger-filled continent with me?" Cecile is teasing, I think.

"I'm doing it now, aren't I?" I tease back.

"This is different." Cecile is serious.

"What's different about it?" I challenge. I'm trying to figure out how she'll reply. Maybe a fighting lift of the left eyebrow. Maybe a shrug. It all depends what phase of the moon her grumpiness is in.

"We are in a car," she says flatly. "We are going to spend the night in a hotel." Sort of a thick crescent, I estimate.

"You're right, Cecile. Absolutely right. There we were in St. Louis in 1826 or so, thinking about running away together where no one knew us just so we could wake up naked next to each other every morning for the rest of our lives. And I said, 'Forget it, Cecile. I'm not going. Cars haven't been invented yet and since there aren't any cars, there isn't any *AAA Tour Book* to advise us about the cheapest hotels. And anyway, they haven't been invented yet, either. So let's stay right here in St. Louis or Boston or wherever we are and become surreptitious spinsters. But I'm not going to let you touch me until there are gas stations that give away maps.'"

"They don't give them away anymore. They sell them."

"Then we'll just have to wait for AAA, which will provide all the maps we'll need for our motoring needs, at no cost beyond our yearly membership fee."

"You mean you'd really go in drag as a man for me?" Cecile is serious again.

I'd actually been thinking that Cecile would be the one to pass as a man, but then I remember the sepia photographs of women in corsets. Cecile would look very sexy in a corset.

"Of course," I say.

"You had to think about it," Cecile accuses. The crescent gets a little thinner.

"Not about you," I say. "Just about what I'd wear."

"You had to think about whether you'd be a man for me." Cecile restates her accusation.

"I would, if that's what we had to do."

"Do you think we would have to?"

"I don't know, Cecile."

"Well, what if one of us was a man. I mean, what if I was a man, really. Would you be heterosexual for me?"

"I guess," I admit.

"You guess?"

"Yeah. I mean, it's kind of hard to imagine, Cecile."

"So, you can imagine being a man, but not being heterosexual for me."

"No, I meant I could imagine pretending to be a man . . ."

"But not pretending to be heterosexual—"

"Cecile, I *would* be heterosexual."

Cecile crosses her arms and moves more firmly into the passenger's seat. She looks out the window. Away from me. Into the flatness.

"Colby!" I scream. "Shut up."

"What?" he finally asks.

"Don't sing so loud."

"Maybe I'll just read my book." His voice sounds raw.

After seven miles of silence, Cecile says, "Yeah, I guess all that open space could make someone crazy."

Sometimes we apologize. Mostly, we just resume.

"How close are we to Childress?" I ask in response.

Cecile gets the map from the floor. "Not far now," she announces. "Where are we?"

"I don't know. Look at the mile markers."

"I don't see any."

By the time we figure out where we are, we are there. In Childress, Texas. Amid its two hotels and a Sonic Burger, on the road that cuts straight through the town. The room is more expensive than the *AAA Tour Book* promised. "There's nothing out here to justify such highway robbery," I complain.

"Maybe that's the point," Cecile says.

We unload the car.

At the Sonic Burger, we order grilled-cheese sandwiches, fries, and shakes. A car hop brings us our food. Maybe we haven't gone back in time to the 1820s, but I'm definitely thinking that a decade or two had left Childress in the dust.

Colby likes his milkshake. He explains how the energy from it is going to his arteries, those little roads inside his body. After a while, I recognize his ramblings as quotes from the *Inside The Human Body* book and tape that has been rotating with *Kids Songs 2.*

"Imagine if we were inside the human body," Colby says excitedly.

"Imagine growing up here," Cecile says, just as I am imagining Colby growing up here. No kids from the Co-op Free School. No alternative bookstores. No bookstores.

"It would be horrible to grow up a dyke here," Cecile proclaims.

"Every place is horrible." I think of my own urban childhood ceilinged by the aspirations for aluminium siding. The boys sweating on the summer sidewalks, making what I thought must be kissing noises whenever I walked by. One girl cursing another for being a faggot when neither of us knew what it meant.

"Yes," Cecile agrees, "but some places are more horrible than others."

I agree more to agree than because I am convinced.

"I wonder if there are any dykes in this town."

"We're here!" Colby screams so loud that for a second I think he's plugged back into *Kids Songs 2.* But the tape player is back at the over-priced hotel.

I keep trying to explain to Colby that he is not a dyke. But he can't seem to accept that Cecile and I are anything that he is not. I explain adulthood/childhood. I talk about gender. I sort of mention sexuality. But none of it sinks in. His logic, or so he told me one day when we were driving across town to get some paint, was that if he came from my body he couldn't really be any different from me. It sounds logical to me.

"Maybe," I say to Cecile, ignoring Colby. As we eat our dinner, I watch for the Childress dyke to go by. I act like I know what I'm looking for, like I'll recognize her when I see her. Cecile is looking for her too.

We find her back in the motel parking lot. She's unpacking a white Landrover. Then her lover comes out from the room to help her. They touch each other on the shoulder and laugh. They are both very tan and have short hair. Short hair that is curly and short hair that is slightly silvery. The moon is rising behind them. They unroll tents and shake them and reroll them. They shake dirt from their tarps. One tosses a canteen to the other. They laugh again.

"We *are* everywhere," Cecile says admiringly.

"Even in Childress," I laugh.

So maybe they aren't really from Childress. Maybe they're from Dallas and just come out here camping. Or maybe they grew up here and escaped and are just back to visit their mothers or a favorite aunt. I don't care why they're here. I don't want to talk with them. It's enough to know that they're here.

Their presence somewhere in this modern 28-unit motel makes us feel safe. Colby is already asleep, sprawled in his own double bed and sandwiched between his two pillows. The door is double-locked, the windows checked, and the bathroom light on, but the dykes are what makes us feel safe.

So safe, it makes us amorous.

There are women I've known who find danger sexy, and once I did, but now I need safety to be passionate. Safety is what I've always craved, what I find astonishingly seductive. Cecile is stroking my left breast, without urgency, like there's no hurry, like we don't have to be on the road at any particular time in the morning. When I lean toward her, she pushes me back gently. "Let me," she says.

I always let Cecile, but there is letting and then there is *letting*. I've never been one to give directions to lovers ("a little to the left, darling"), so I don't start telling Cecile what to do. But that doesn't mean there aren't voices somewhere inside my body using my arteries like telephone wires, demanding *more of this, less of that.* Yet every time the *this* and the *that* are different, which is the pragmatic reason I never let these voices sneak outside my own body. One voice would get out and dominate all the others, as if this voice were best and true. Eventually, the voices recede, like the last lights of the waning moon, and I am full with Cecile.

Tonight, in a motel in Childress, Texas, Cecile is asking me not to wait for those voices to gradually dissipate. She is telling me that I am safe, that our passion is certain, that the moon will always be in our sky.

She is telling me that we have all night. She is pushing me back on the polyester pillows while her fingers continue to nibble at my left breast. Usually, my right breast would be jealous and assertive by now, my body rolling to make it prominent. But tonight I am patient. Safe.

Safe even when Cecile bites at my left nipple. Then again, harder or softer, it is hard to judge which. Safe even as Cecile smoothes down my body, pulling both pillows from under my head to under my hips. Safe even as she pushes the sheet to one side, my foot caught in a tangle. Safe even as she kneels between my legs and then sits on her heels, looking at me for a long silence.

Safe as I am wet with wanting and with being wanted. Safe with Cecile's head between my thighs, her tongue inside and outside and all sides and both her thumbs and all her fingers spreading and closing and stroking the places her tongue has just been or is just going. Safe although I can't tell the difference between her tongue and her fingers, between her touching and my being touched. Safe although she is on her heels again, kneeling between my shaking legs. My ass arches off the pillows, my pelvis sucks at the air for her fingers and tongue. Her face shines wet, reflected in the bathroom light.

Safe even as she is beside me, pushing her body ever so slightly against me. My arteries sing, off-key and loudly. Cecile strokes my left breast again, softly, almost carelessly. A sudden pinch. Then slow strokes again. It is going to be a long night, Cecile promises me again.

We only oversleep slightly in the morning, getting up early enough to see our fellow dykes in the parking lot. They are laughing and packing their white Landrover. We laugh, too, wondering if their lovemaking was as passionate as our own.

They are refolding their tent when the two men join them. Each man hugs a woman. The women giggle, their laughter for each other dissolved and domesticated. The men finish packing the Landrover. We try not to watch them, try not to watch the men touch the women.

We are nervous in retrospect.

Cecile wants to leave, not even go to the coffee shop for breakfast.

I want to stay, more than ever. I want to walk up and down Route 287, looking cool as James Dean, Kerouac, all of the Grateful Dead. But I no longer want to be them, not even them as characters in movies or novels or songs. In order to see the real dyke of Childress, Texas, I'm going to have to be a character in a lesbian pulp novel, or a not-yet-made-for-TV movie, or a dyke country-and-western lament. I have to be fated to meet the Childress, Texas dyke. I'm not going to fall in love with her or anything (even as a character, I'm dedicated to Cecile), but we are going to have a few poignant exchanges which will bring one of us epiphany, heal our secret scars, or give us insight into our futures. Or maybe I can be a character in a more subtle genre, a literary attempt in which I'll notice the labrys in her ear and we'll smile evocatively at each other, across the Sonic Burger counter. Or an independent film in which I'll lipstick a lesbian symbol in the Sonic Burger bathroom and she'll smile knowingly at it after I've left, into the forever-altered mirror.

"Let's go," Cecile insists.

"Cecile," I say, "somewhere in this town of 5,500 is a girl-woman who knows she's different and doesn't know why. She needs to see us, Cecile, just as badly as we need to see her." I don't mention last night. "She needs to see us so that she knows she has a chance."

"You sure have a big city ego." Cecile might be developing a twang. Her eyebrows arch, almost evocatively.

"What do you mean?"

"I mean you think you have to be from New York or Miami to be a dyke. Maybe there's a whole flock of dykes in this town. Maybe there's a commune even you haven't heard of. Maybe the mayor is a dyke.

Maybe the high school principal is a dyke. Maybe everyone knows and thinks it's just great to be a dyke in Childress, Texas."

Cecile is unusually shrill. Yes, she has more phases than any moon. And yes, she is infinitely less predictable than any moon, cycling from full to crescent to full and then half and then full and then crescent in less than an hour. But her moon is made of grumpiness; she is hardly ever shrill. It's her shrillness that keeps me from pointing out that last night *she* was the one who pitied anyone growing up in Childress, Texas, and I was the one who said it was hard to grow up anywhere. Still, I don't like being called egotistical.

"I'm just saying it's hard," I say. Despite my best efforts, I add, "like I said last night."

"It is hard," Cecile agrees, acting ignorant of my transgression.

"Let's go," Cecile says again, in a sort of shrill twang.

In the car, I am driving. Colby is complaining, waiting for breakfast. Cecile is listening to the Bonnie Raitt tape, only this morning she fast-forwards past "Real Man" into "Nobody's Girl."

The flat road stretches before us. It gives me nothing to define myself against. It makes me feel insignificant. Unsafe.

"Switch that tape, will you?" I ask Cecile. "I'm a little weary of heterosexuality this morning."

"Oh, sure." Cecile sarcastically flips through our tapes. "Which of the popular singers who are totally out there for us as dykes would you like to hear? Maybe k.d. lang? How about Tracy Chapman? Maybe Madonna? Madonna's girlfriend?"

"Cecile, just put in Ferron or Alix Dobkin or somebody."

"Can't."

"Why not?"

"Broken."

"All of them?"

"Overuse."

Cecile's attack of monosyllablism lapses into an attack of silence. Even Bonnie Raitt has shut up. Only Colby's voice comes in spurts from the back seat, flat as the land that stretches in all directions. *Desperado. Colorado. Wild and wooly West.*

Cecile and I are speaking by Amarillo, where we breakfast. We don't see the white Landrover. We don't talk about dykes. Or about last night. Or about illusions of safety.

"How far is Albuquerque?" I ask her.

She looks at the distance map. "Two hundred eighty-eight miles," she says, after adding up numbers.

"I hear there's a good women's bookstore there," I say. "Maybe we can spring for some replacement tapes."

Cecile agrees, closing that last distance between us, reestablishing the safety that we sometimes forget is dependent on each other.

Desert Scars

Menstruation And The Painted Desert

"We're almost there," Cecile announces.

The land has been turning pinker and my softest jeans have been getting tighter all day.

"How you feeling?" Cecile asks.

"Cramps," I answer.

"A shower will help. Soon," Cecile promises. "Soon, we'll be there."

There is Holbrook, Arizona. I'm thinking that a shower might help. And I'm also thinking how unfair it is and feeling sorry for myself. I have waited my whole life to be here, and now I'm going to be here doubled over.

I only menstruate six or seven times a year, a lunar cycle for some moon of Jupiter or Saturn, I suppose. Oddly irregular, worse since Colby's birth. Strange, Cecile thought, how easily I became alternatively inseminated despite the irregular cycles. I found nothing odd about the easy conception, easy pregnancy, easy birth. Nothing odd except the baby's gender.

I never thought I'd give birth to a boy. Never thought I'd live to see the Painted Desert.

"Tell me about the Painted Desert," Cecile coaxes.

"What about it?"

"What you think about it."

"I haven't seen it yet."

"I know that," Cecile feigns patience. It is not one of her strengths. "So why don't you tell me about your fifth grade report on it?"

"Fourth grade."

"Whatever."

"You're not really interested," I accuse. "You just want to take my mind off my abdomen."

"I'm interested," Colby perks up.

"Only because you can't imagine I was ever in the fourth grade."

"Watch out, Colby," Cecile warns. "She's totally grumpy."

"I am not grumpy, Cecile," I protest. She knows perfectly well that she is the only one in this car who ever gets grumpy. I get moody. She gets grumpy.

"You were in the fourth grade before I was born, weren't you?" Colby asks.

"Yes."

"But I still lived in your stomach, right?"

"In a way."

"So, I really have been a fourth grader already, right?"

"Do you want to hear about my report on the Painted Desert or not?"

"Will I have to write reports when I'm in the fourth grade?" Colby asks. I interpret this as meaning he wants to hear about my report.

"Well, the Painted Desert isn't painted, and it isn't really a desert, either. I don't remember much else. I got a C-minus on my report."

"At least you didn't fail," Colby reminds me. How did such an optimist ever live inside me? Or maybe he's only smoothing the way for his own fourth grade career.

"Why did you get a C-minus?" Cecile asks, knowing very well why. But since I'm distracting myself, I pretend she's forgotten the story I told her when we first looked at maps and planned our trip, me insisting that we stop and see the Painted Desert.

"Because it didn't have a government. Because everyone else in the class did Italy or Israel or Ireland or Indonesia or India. They had charts with gross national products and natural resources and populations. They had flags and dates of wars and famous men. I had pink shades of chalk that were supposed to look like layers of sediment."

"So, that's why you like pink," Colby says, as if in explanation.

"Yes," I agree. What I don't add is that pink seemed the only color magical enough to transform the gray world I lived in, that I carefully shaded the pinks and thought of them as scars produced by centuries of survival. And what I especially don't add, but what Cecile must remember from the first time I told her this story—Colby safely asleep while we looked at maps on our kitchen table—was how I tried to create that pink world of mesas for myself.

Although my teacher, Miss Paterson, wasn't impressed with my report, Iris definitely was. Iris was much more impressionable that Miss Patterson, and definitely cuter. She'd failed her geography report, even though she'd picked a place with a government (Iraq, I think), because she wasn't yet fluent in English. I thought she should have gotten a good grade just for the crescent moon she had stenciled on her flag, but Miss Paterson said she'd gotten the wrong flag and everything.

Next, Miss Paterson was having us memorize the flags of countries of the world. Iris invited me over to help her with our homework.

I've tried to remember how we developed our routine, our scene, many times since the fourth grade. Who said what when. Or even where we got the ideas.

The desert had to be hot, we knew that, so we moved all the lamps, even the heavy glass one, from the rest of the small apartment into Iris' room. We arranged them as carefully as we could to get them to shine in our faces. The people in the desert wore robes—we'd seen pictures from the *Children's Illustrated Bible* in the school library. So we stripped and draped Iris' sheets around our bodies, making sure one of our bare shoulders always protruded. The desert was magical, we felt that. So we daydreamed rituals in which we removed each other's robes and showered in (pretend) blood that we lathered and rubbed on each other's (real) fourth-grade bodies. We positioned ourselves so that the familiarly unfamiliar region my mother called crotch and we didn't call anything—that region without flag or government or famous men—began to tingle. This tingling was our magical symbol that soon we would enter the world of women and begin our own menstruation, contributing to the blood needed to shower and lather and rub ourselves in the desert. This tingling was produced as our blood seeped downward into our desert caves braceleted with varying shades of pink, pushing to come out into the desert sun.

The desert had only women. We made that part up.

Our desert had only the two of us. We were the last girls who hadn't yet become women. We rubbed and lathered each other toward the culmination that we thought was menstruation.

Eventually, of course, we got caught.

Iris' mother must have noticed the lamps never put back exactly right no matter how hard we tried, or the sheets all confused, or something. Or maybe she just came home from work early because she had cramps. But one afternoon, right in the middle of our ritual, she walked right into Iris' bedroom. She screamed in the universal language of mothers of daughters. She unraveled us from our bedspread robes and screamed louder. She threw my clothes at Iris and Iris' clothes at me. There was no blood, but she screamed like there was. And then she threw the glass lamp. Only the light bulb broke, but I managed to step on it and cut my foot. It was the first time there had been any real blood. It was disappointingly more red than pink.

It wasn't the first time that I learned that loving girls was going to be difficult and confusing, and maybe even dangerous. But I was determined not to give it up.

What I did give up was looking for Iris. I found out her mother had transferred her to a private religious school and was relieved to hear that at least she was alive. What I also gave up was the idea that menstruation was a holy act of spirituality and sexuality. I learned it was messy and sometimes painful, something to avoid during cross-country trips and while wearing favorite jeans.

But I didn't give up my desire to see the Painted Desert.

The entrance flies government flags, including the flag of the government park service. What I want to see is annexed to the main attraction of the Petrified Forest. Colby doesn't understand what *petrified* means, despite Cecile's almost-patient explanations, and he is also beginning to have doubts that he understands *forest*. It looks like a lot of loose rocks. It is crowded with people wearing Grand Canyon T-shirts and expensive sneakers.

In the annex of the Painted Desert, I'm wondering why it doesn't match my fourth-grade rendition. It is too blue. Blue, like the favorite color of Cecile's ex-husband. There are no women in robes. No Iris. Only Cecile, my grumpy lover, trying to keep us cheerful.

"Do you want aspirin?" she offers.

My cramps, like old scars, ache in the dry, crowded air.

"Let's go," Cecile suggests. We do not protest.

The car feels smaller than ever. My head bangs the glove compartment. Cecile is driving and massaging me. I'm feeling dizzy. Claustrophobic.

"I need to get out of this car."

Some side highway. Too many miles. Deep into the mauve mesas. Flat-topped striped mountains. Into the Little Painted Desert, a county park of Navaho County. No bathrooms. Down a path. Alone. While Colby and Cecile wander across another path.

The sun is sliding toward twilight. The mesas turn pink. Light and dark and every pastel and pure hue of pink. Intermixed with an electric blue like no one's eyes. And the most comforting shade of gray.

Behind a slab of sand compressed into rock, I pull down my jeans and squat. It is hot. My body is hotter. I give birth to a perfectly healthy menstrual clot, rich red, irregularly shaped. I do not rub it into my skin. Or into the sand. I leave it there like a little flag, a little country. Maybe the vultures will eat it. And I walk back to Cecile and Colby, almost standing straight, almost as if I am not scarred.

The Face Of The Mohave

The Mohave is high desert, not like my dreams of desert. Flat sands as open as West Texas, with cactus as huge as a small country. Instead, it recalls my dreams last night of the mesas: not dreams, really, but permanent postcards inscribed on the insides of my eyelids. More blue than I'd imagined, but also indelibly pink. Today, in the Mohave, the radiance is muted. The pinks are tan, the mauves are beige, the blues are browns.

There are rocks like litter, mixed with the real litter of bottles and cellophane alongside the state highway. Nothing decomposes. Nothing rots. Only blows.

We had been worried about the heat. We had filled two jugs with water, checked the tires, and filled up with gas. Our Florida-thin blood reacted only to the altitude and lack of humidity. We were used to the heat.

The high winds buffet the small car.

"Pull over," Cecile instructs. I do. On the side of the road a small sign says Rattlesnake Wash.

"Stay in the car," Cecile directs.

"I have to pee," Colby announces.

"Stay in the car," I say to Cecile, casually, as if her fear of rattlesnakes is a casual matter. I listen for hissing above the hush of the wind, watching the ground carefully while Colby pees behind a low bush. Watching Colby's urine, not scattered by the wind or soaked into the thirsty ground, but puddling. Then elongating to dent the dirt like a dull blade in flesh.

Huge hills linger at a distance I cannot judge. Bare except for deep cuts. Jagged. Unhealing.

Flash floods. Rain that ravages. Water that can't be absorbed. Rattlesnake Wash. Dry now, hot as a mirror. And as silent. There is only the incessant hiss of the wind. The sign rattling.

I rush Colby back into the car.

We sit in our metal space, waiting for the wind to calm, unable to get a radio station.

I catch my own eye in the sideview mirror. It is surrounded by shocking whiteness. It isn't that I've forgotten that I'm Caucasian, or even that my tan doesn't seem as impressive in the Southwest as it did in Florida. What shocks is the absence of dried pink. The absence of thin crusted lines like a patternless web across my checks. Across my forehead. Surrounding my eyes.

The glass was sharp. There were many pieces demanding to be chosen. The mirror had smashed exquisitely, like cheap glass always does. Glass not spun from sand. Synthetic. Something man-made. A convenient piece large enough and almost oval, fitting smoothly in my left hand. So I could watch myself. My right hand as steady as if I were applying make-up. Eyeliner rather than rouge. Slender cuts in my adolescent flesh. Careful. Controlled. Wiping excess blood with tissues I wet with my tongue. Careful. It was important to achieve the tragic beauty of suffering and not the puffy ugliness of rejection.

When she saw me like that, my face etched with anguish and only slightly swollen, it made no difference that she was willing to tell me about. Perhaps she confided in her new boyfriend. Though I sensed they didn't talk much, and even if they did, this would not be something she would tell him about.

I told my mother I ran into a window.

I told Cecile about it and I laughed. She didn't. She asked me what I told my mother. I couldn't tell her that I lied to my mother. Cecile's mother was sleeping in the next room, trying to recover from chemotherapy.

Tucked in the car, I change my view to the rearview mirror, checking to see if the wind or the driver is controlling that blue pick-up truck coming up the highway.

"Did you see any snakes out there?" Cecile finally asks.

"Not a one. It must be too windy." But the wind is dying now, transforming itself into a strong breeze.

We are still driving in the high desert when a rainstorm without thunder erupts. Instant rivers cut the shimmering land.

Theories Of Men

"It's just like a man," Cecile says.

"Don't genderize," I tell her.

"What?"

"Genderize," I explain, "You know, generalize about gender."

"You've been reading too much of that theory shit since we got here," Cecile complains.

Since is six weeks. *Here* is Berkeley. Or Oakland, depending on where on our street we are standing. Depending on whether I'm trying to be a student at an exclusive private women's college or at an equally exclusive but sprawling public university. Depending on whether Colby is at kindergarten or home.

There must be some theory to explain the boundaries between Berkeley and Oakland, but I haven't figured it out yet. Colby hasn't yet figured out that both Berkeley and Oakland are cities, and that two different cities can both be in the state of California and that San Francisco is not a different country like Iran and China and the other places the kids in his class are from. "California is a state like Florida," I tell him, over and over. He hasn't yet grasped the theory of geography.

To me, Cecile says, "I just don't understand what you see in all that theory stuff." She sounds more perplexed than critical, more apologetic than disapproving.

I could answer, *Theory saved my life*, but I don't. If I say it out loud, I'll have to admit it's overdramatic. But even melodrama has its truths.

The first time I read Marxist theory, I cried. Cried with release. Suddenly there was an explanation for my hatred of those girls from the suburbs who had houses with yards, who had fathers with careers, who had mothers that picked them up in station wagons from tumbling lessons. There were explanations like class conflict, dialectical materialism, and workers who didn't own the modes of production. And if I didn't understand all of it very clearly, it was clearly more comforting than suspecting I was simply mean-spirited, envious, and evil.

And even if it wasn't spiritual enough, it was better than all those religious tracts that counseled patience and worship of supernatural beings. It was a religion of ourselves. And even if it wasn't womanly enough, it was better than all those ladies' journals that prescribed thrift and devotion to invisible husbands. It was a journalism of reality.

The idea that it might not be all my fault was addictive. From Marx, I went to college. I integrated my strange spirituality with rational thought. I disregarded all maleness because, after all, Philo Sophia was a woman. I took a seminar in Plato's *Symposium* and learned that homosexuality was natural. I learned enough to graduate, but I did not. I dropped out.

And now I am back.

But while I was gone from Philo Sophia, she went on without me. Like an old lover who continues with her life, Philo Sophia traveled, changed residences, and took up with other people, as if I never existed. For fifteen years I'd been thinking of her as she had been, mentioning her during lunchtime discussions with potentially lecherous bosses, remembering her during long languid talks with Cecile. For me, she remained concerned with being, time, space, appearances, and reality. She cavorted with a bunch of mostly dead Germans whose names mostly began with *H*: Hegel, Heidegger, Husserl, Habermas. I remember the day Heidegger died, someone wrote it on the board in the classroom. And Habermas is still alive, writing two-thousand-page books that are long-winded protests. Now, Philo Sophia has other favorites.

She abandoned Germany for France and is less concerned about existence than expression. They call it semiotics, which sounds slightly sinister and more male than being, time, or reality ever did. Six weeks in Berkeley and Oakland and I am talking about texts, not books; about deconstruction, not dialectics. I am listening to lectures assuming my knowledge of Foucault, Derrida, Lacan, and Lyotard. I listen to Philo Sophia described not as a muse, but as a slut. No longer a goddess, never was. By nature unfaithful. She's a fragment, a construction, a discourse.

I never should have left her.

Still, even in this transformed state, she's seductive. Which is why I tell Cecile not to genderize.

I did not need to wait fifteen years and travel twenty-seven hundred miles to learn that it is ridiculous to make generalized statements about gender. I've had too many perfectly womanly women fuck me over to believe that women were a generalized good. And if I'd believed men were a generalized evil, I would have abandoned Colby on a slanted patch of ground to overheat in the subtropical sun.

No, Philo Sophia in her modern incarnation—or more accurately, her postmodern mechanization—insists that gender is not even a category, and neither is anything like "sexual orientation." After modernism, Philo Sophia eschews all labels. To be her follower, one must be relentlessly trendy.

In the Technologies of Sexuality course I learn that all sexual expression is fluid, unmappable, and contradictory. I learn that to say *homosexual* is ridiculous. If one said it at all, it could only be an adjective. And it had to be heavily qualified by other adjectives. Because, after all, homosexuals did not even exist as a category until the nineteenth century. And lesbians, later.

In the Theories of Feminism course I learn that gender is a construct. I learn that to say *woman* is ludicrous. Women are too different from each other to be a consistent class. And woman is a changing concept throughout history.

But even though I chastise Cecile according to Philo Sophia's new fashions, I'm not a true believer. I don't feel trendy enough. I don't have the vocabulary. I have a feeling it was not meant for me.

Not meant for resumers. For that is what I am labeled here, with a special scholarship for my special category, a student resuming her education. As if I had just stepped out of the drawing room to check on why the help is late with tea. Having scolded the maids for dawdling, I return and the conversation resumes.

But it's a different conversation. With different participants. The women—I have to bite my tongue to keep from calling them girls—all shine with the patina of privilege. They are all sweet and all serious. They are multicolored but not multicultured. Their culture is high culture, that closed world of success. They look like they could order in elegant restaurants but not work in the kitchens, like they would prevail in a lacrosse tournament, but not survive a knife fight.

I crossed the country to come here because I wanted an all-women's college. And to be honest, because I wangled a scholarship. But now the school's well-kept grounds seem like an antebellum womb, and I feel like a poor relation.

So, I read and I read. I read like I taught myself: with passion. But what I am reading seems less like words than like symbols. I read more parentheses, more slashes, and more italics in one week than I'd ever read before in my whole life. I read words like *di(va)lution*; words like *erratic/erotic*; words like *illisible*. I read more theory by more women than I ever did before, adorned with these parentheses, slashes, and italics. But the theories are the theories of men. The same preoccupations. The same cleverness and rhetoric. And sometimes it seems worse than the theories of men I'd read long ago. As if Marx had never existed. As if only Europe had ever existed. These theories smell like the theories of men, like the theories of men in control. They still smell like divide and conquer to me. And who gets divided and who gets conquered isn't different enough to make a difference.

I want to say this in one of my classes. But every time I open my mouth, which isn't often, I learn that the consequences of speaking are brutal. This time, the class is feminist theory. It's never called feminist philosophy, although whether this is from respect or disrespect I cannot tell. I've left the womb of women's education for the gender diversity of a great state institution. Of course, there are only women in my class. But the question today is, as always, Are women a class?

Whatever women have in common is painstakingly erased each week in our windowless seminar room. Each student invokes women we think are not present in that room: dishwashers, prostitutes, slaves, illiterates, farmworkers, rug weavers in Kashmir. We each do our homework, underlining the assigned texts, making notes in the margins. We are quick to condemn when anyone's conclusions are less than universal. We pick at other women's biases like they are scabs we cannot allow to heal.

And I scratch too. For I have been excluded from the definition of woman by too many women. I have had the wrong lovers, the wrong accent, the wrong job, the wrong family, the wrong address. And I have witnessed others being excluded by definition, as if *woman* could not mean *black* and so woman must be modified. The standards shift: my skin has been too white, my eyes too blue, my clothes too accommodating, my relationship too traditional. The standards reshift: my skin has been pocked by poverty, my eyes red from drugs, my clothes torn, and my relationships too outrageous. I have been on the wrong side of every privilege, because there is no right side.

Still, I think there is something special in that word: *woman*. Something irreducible. Blame it on the residual Hegel (the universe tends toward synthesis). Blame it on the first blushes of women's studies (the universe belongs to women). Blame it on my mother, on all those schoolgirl crushes, on lovers who knew how to bite and how to cuddle. Blame it on Cecile.

So although I scratch, I scratch tenderly, a little afraid of the blood. And in this class, I come to represent the naiveté of feminism before it was a theory, the exclusionary days when feminist anthologies did not include men, the time when there were posters but not prestigious journals. I am fifteen years older than any other student, ten years older than the professor—who calls herself a facilitator. But I never speak personally. No one does.

Until our theoretical topic of the week is pornography. We are assigned the writings of sex workers, of Linda Lovelace, of MacKinnon and Dworkin, of sex radicals. It is not a topic I want to discuss theoretically, especially with women I hardly know. Yet for the first time women start to speak about their own lives, each one revealing the time a boyfriend had taken her to see the movie *Deep Throat*. Each woman feels differently about it, but each woman tells her tale.

Except me. I'm the dyke who never had any boyfriend to take her to any movie. I'm the one who doesn't fit. The one who deviates from this universal experience. The dishwasher, prostitute, slave, illiterate, farmworker, rug weaver in Kashmir. The exception that trashes the rule. But no one is invoking me.

I open my mouth. I have not decided whether or not I will depart from theory or depart from personal revelation.

"That movie was probably before your time," the student next to me says.

Now I am going to have to address ageism. Before, I was only going to say that it might be different for lesbians. I was only going to say that some relationships to pornography might be more complex than others. I was only going to say that I had never seen *any* movie with *any* boyfriend.

I was not going to say I had been a prostitute. That I was once even a dishwasher.

But I don't say anything because the same woman next to me who had just erased my existence is shoving me under the table.

It is dark under here, shielded from fluorescent lights. It feels safe. I think we are going to continue our conversation. A new intimacy.

She grabs my hand.

"It's an earthquake," she says.

I feel nothing. Have felt nothing. I try not to feel ridiculous. I am cool. Cooler than cool. This is California. These things happen all the time. I reassure myself, since no else is talking.

Then I see the corner of the room, where the floor caresses the wall, quiver as if to break the embrace. Then the corner rolls again and my stomach rolls with it. Then someone screams, echoing their womanly voice off the underside of the table.

I do not see my life flash before me. Instead, I pull it into me. Nothing will happen. I absolutely refuse to die without holding hands with Cecile and Colby.

There are theories to explain earthquakes. Theories of stress and plates and pressure. A tremblor. The ground grinds and things slip from the sky.

There are theories of measurement. They agree that this one shall be numbered at 7.0. There are theories of prediction. They can't agree that any are accurate.

Outside of the feminist theory class, out from under the table and into the street, I can see smoke. I can hear sirens. I can feel Cecile and Colby on their way to get me.

There are aftershocks. There is a picture Colby draws full of red lines like lightning. There are jammed telephone lines. There is the radio. With batteries.

There is news that the bridge between us and San Francisco collapsed. There is news that eighteen blocks of double-decker freeway one mile from our house has collapsed. There is news that the Marina is collapsing with fire.

There is news and news and news. A woman in Santa Cruz screams while the rescue workers try to get her friend out from the rubble of a store. The same woman in Santa Cruz screams when the rescue workers are told to quit their efforts. The news doesn't say that *friend* means *lover*.

Some things you know without being told.

The theories name the faults: San Andreas, Hayward, Calaveras, Seal Cove, Los Positas. The theories call them faults, like there is something wrong, like they should not be there. Like they need explanations.

In Technologies of Sexuality and Theories of Feminism, we talk about the earthquake. The very ground on which we stand is fragmented, uncertain, fissured. A sort of geophysical postmodernism. Everyone seems satisfied. But they are still nervous. It is not trendy to be nervous. Therapists at both schools offer their services gratis to people coping with disaster anxieties. The woman who held my hand, who said I was too old to know what she meant, never returns to class.

Colby gets a book and tape on earthquakes. The biggest. The most damage. The strongest. He memorizes facts and repeats them. Like an incantation.

Like I once repeated *class conflict, dialectical materialism, modes of production.* Until I couldn't find all of my mother in those terms. Until I couldn't find any of the women I loved in those words. Until I admitted I didn't know what they meant.

Cecile reads the newspapers for predictions. Earthquakes replace rattlesnakes as her favorite fear. At night, she listens for rumblings instead of hissings.

Wrapped in our pink bedspread, I snuggle next to Cecile as if my body heat can counteract her anxious chill. I look out the long windows at our backyard. The shaken dirt still nourishes the mesa-red poppies on thick green vines caressing our miracle of a tree. Not a eucalyptus tree with peeling bark, or a sequoia with furrowed bark, but a genuine palm tree with pineapple bark and tropical hair. A palm tree. Date or Royal or California—it was hard to tell, but definitely a palm tree.

I wonder how this palm tree survives this cool Alcatraz air, fog thicker than smoke. I wonder how this palm tree survives these tremors that shake the rich California dirt from its roots.

There must be theories that justify palm trees, but they do not explain this tree's survival.

The theories do not explain earthquakes.

And the theories do not explain lesbians. Or women.

Because even when they do, they don't.

The earth shifts.

Women love women.

I love Cecile.

No theories can explain that (away).

Home(less)

"Hundreds homeless after earthquake," Cecile reads out loud. The people who were homeless before the earthquake don't count anymore, if they ever did. What Cecile reads isn't a headline, but just another title to another article about postearthquake life in the *San Francisco Chronicle*.

I prefer the *Oakland Tribune*, not because of its comparative journalistic qualities, but because of my new regional loyalty. Once I learned that it was necessary to distinguish between the East Bay (Berkeley and Oakland), the South Bay (Santa Cruz), the North Bay (Marin), and the City by the Bay (San Francisco), I decided that the East Bay must be superior in all respects, except the respects that distinguished the Bay Area from the rest of California, from the rest of the country.

But I do not read the *Oakland Tribune*, either. I hardly ever read newspapers. I can never fold them neatly enough and no matter how I fold them the black ink gets all over my white hands. Cecile reads me the most interesting snippets, from every section except the editorials, which she never reads. If I'm interested in those, I can listen to the public radio announcer every morning who first reads all the local editorials and then a few from the *New York Times*.

Even if I read the paper, I wouldn't read the *New York Times*. I'd read the *East Bay Express*. Sometimes I do, asking Cecile to fold it for me. It's a free weekly that doesn't sully itself with daily indexes and government proclamations. It's more about everyday life than that. The main stories were always the best: there was one about what kind of guy Black Panther Huey Newton was (not very nice); one about suburban neighborhood gangs (meaner than expected); one about the drought's effects on the birds and bugs of Mount Diablo (they were disappearing). All first-person stuff, timely but not too timely. I could leave the paper around for a week and it was still worth reading. It was almost worth smudging my hands.

The smaller articles were about local politics, local movies and local personalities. I wait for a big first person feature written by a homeless person, or some journalistic exploration of homelessness. It must be passé. The closest I get is a letter by some guy who reports he never leaves his home without a roll of quarters, dispensing it until its gone, and then just saying, Sorry.

I wonder how often this guy goes out. I can't afford ten dollars a day—that's three hundred dollars a month! Yet what I admire about the guy is his plan. He's got one. I need one.

I settle on gender. I will give money only to women. There are fewer of them, and they need it more. I don't announce my plan, but I act on it. It makes me feel secure to have some standards when I face the panhandlers.

When I was a panhandler, I had no standards. I gleaned advice, but when it wasn't contradictory, it was dangerous. I was never very successful. There were white hippie chicks on every corner then, all of us barefoot, most of us drugged. We were trying to trade on our innocence, but I didn't have much left and there were better ways to make money. Their skirts got longer, mine got shorter. We started to live in different worlds within the same city, where the dirtiness and desperateness of every other city was exceeded. We called it New York.

Now I wonder what ever happened to those girls, especially the ones with the babies named Sunshine and Moonbeam. Twenty years ago I looked at those diaperless babies with such derision, knowing I'd never have children, knowing I'd never be knocked up by some guy no matter how gentle he appeared, no matter how long his hair, no matter how much he looked like a woman.

Now I'm parking in front of a trendy Berkeley bookstore, lucky to have a space during prime Saturday shopping time, knowing my own six-year old is home with my lover who not only looks like a woman but actually is one. I'm looking for a particular book for a class. I'm a good student, a resumer, acting like those twenty years never existed.

It will only take me a minute. But that's not the reason I don't put a quarter in the parking meter. I am not a risky person. I am neither careless nor carefree. I learned to be reponsible, to have a state job, a child, a lover for more than three months. I am counted on and accountable. I am a good citizen who doesn't break the law casually. Only conscientiously.

I even have a quarter. But I can't bring myself to root around in my wallet for it. Not with all these homeless people as witnesses. Better I should give it to them. But which one? I can't do that, either. There are too many of them. And they're all men.

Like so many other people, when I don't know what to do, I pretend I'm not doing anything. I pretend none of it exists: not the car, not the parking meter, not the men on the street, not my wallet, not my conscience. All that exists are my legs and the bookstore door. If anyone asks me for change, I don't hear.

Inside, the book I need isn't shelved under the sign that says WOMEN. The women's section is big, and it takes me a while to look through the titles because I look even when I know it isn't the book I need for my class. I once heard a woman here complaining about this section: she thought it was ghettoizing. To me, it's convenience. The gay section is small and only has books by men. They shelve the lesbians with WOMEN, so I never have to go anywhere else. It's like home. Everything I need is here.

But the book I want isn't. Perhaps it is in SOCIOLOGY. POLITICS? I go up the ramp to those sections. The books seem more expensive. They have titles on the Australian government, on socialist technology, on population patterns. There are even a few books on homelessness. But they don't have the book I want.

I could ask. I don't. I could be wrong about the title, wrong about the author's name, about how it's pronounced. I'm ignorant and uncool and afraid I don't really belong in this bookstore. The people who work here were probably all successful panhandlers, probably all refugees from the Haight in 1968, probably all have kids who are in college at the right age. I leave the store.

Of course, I have a parking ticket. I unlock my car door, pull the ticket from the windshield, toss it on the floorboard. I don't react. Nothing exists. Even the crowd of homeless people is gone. Or maybe it never was a crowd. Maybe it was two men, three at the most. Maybe not even homeless. Maybe they were happy campers, walking their way from New York to the Pacific, stopping in Berkeley to rest outside a bookstore.

The fine is fourteen dollars. The net worth of my embarrassment is $13.75. For a quarter, I could have avoided this. The city, this puny too-cool city, gets what would have been better given to the men on the street.

I'll go get Colby. People never panhandle me when he's clutching my hand. I wonder why not.

I wonder if the city uses any of its parking fine money for the homeless. Probably not. It seems mostly left to churches, or a few citizens' groups—people who panhandled in the sixties and now have three-hundred-thousand-dollar houses. People who used to staff the food tent in People's Park. Actually, it was a camper on blocks. They called it People's Café, and I like to think that they served fresh ground coffee, scones of hand-milled flour, organic oranges cut into paper-thin wedges, and Calistoga water. Of course, they didn't. But I did like to think it, until the city brought in equipment at 5:00 A.M. to haul the trailer away. There were letters of protest in the *East Bay Express*. Later, an article. But the city didn't relent. Now some guy cooks hamburgers out there on Saturday afternoons. It just isn't the same. At least the city left the bathrooms.

Colby and I are walking past the port-o-lets that ring People's Park. I'm telling him it isn't much farther. It isn't, but we've already walked too far. Just because I didn't want to park anywhere that had a meter. I'm trying to make it up to him by being entertaining. He's not listening, only complaining. He's getting past the age where I can persuade him that everything is just another adventure.

He still loves feathers, though. I hope he never gets too old to love feathers. We find a beautiful one on the sidewalk. He rushes away from me to get it first. We stop, admire it together. It is long with slate blue-black vanes. Colby pronounces it beautiful. Finding feathers is one of the things I taught this child, during long toddler walks through fields and on beaches. There's a jar we brought all the way from Florida, unbroken, that displays his varied collection. Every addition is special. For feathers are lucky, we both agree. Omens of change and freedom. Maybe my day will improve.

"Put it in your pocket," I tell him.

He obeys, but is taking it out again when he cries, "Look, another one."

And this one is larger than the other. A tail feather probably. Bent like it had flown far and wide.

"How lucky we are today," I say.

Even People's Park looks beautiful as we walk. The gardens are flowering, as always. The fog is dispersed. Everyone seems happy.

"Look, more!" Colby is excited to find three more feathers.

"Someone must have lost their collection," I say. There are feather earrings, feather masks, feather hats for sale on Telegraph Avenue. There must be a feather wholesaler somewhere.

We're at the border of the park when we see the bird. The dead bird. With its bloody feathers. Slate black-blue.

"What kind is it?" Colby asks.

I don't know, but I say sparrow anyway. I don't even know if there are sparrows in California.

"I think it's a starling," he says.

I forgot that Colby is learning about birds in kindergarten, that Colby collects facts like he collects feathers.

"Maybe," I admit.

Inside the bookstore, Colby wants to find a bird book so that we can decide what kind of bird the dead bird was. What the hell does it matter? I want to ask him. But I am supposed to be nurturing his inquisitive nature. I lie instead. "They don't have any bird books here."

At least not in the women's section. The lesbians aren't in the women's section in this store. They're segregated out into a section that doesn't have a name—or at least not yet. A section squashed between WOMEN'S STUDIES and MEN'S STUDIES.

"I can't believe this huge bookstore doesn't have bird books," Colby says, too loudly. I'm afraid one of the people who works here will come over and try to help us.

"They don't have the book I need, either," I tell him.

It's a long walk home. The fog starts to drift in, making me feel like I'm a mother in a spooky movie. But at least we don't find any more feathers.

Cecile must not know how tired my Saturday has made me. She doesn't have supper ready. She doesn't feel like shopping, like talking. We drink coffee. I heat up pizza for Colby.

I nag Cecile until she'll talk to me. I don't have the book I need to read, so I want to talk about some sort of feminist or lesbian issue. Cecile wants to talk about work.

When Cecile worked at the feminist art collective, she never wanted to talk about it with me. I always thought it would be terribly interesting. Now that Cecile is working as an art librarian for the university, she wants to talk about it. It's terribly boring.

Cecile complains that she's being treated like shit. I'm not surprised, only surprised that she seems surprised. Maybe she worked with the women's collective too long—the pay was shit but the idea wasn't. Still, after that she was a student. If anything could prepare one for being treated like shit, it's being a student, especially one of those resuming students.

Maybe Cecile has just forgotten what work is really like. And how lucky she is to have a job at all.

I hate it when I think like that. The grateful girl. "You're so lucky," people said to me, calling it luck that I might have a chance at what they took for granted.

When Cecile's conversation shifts to someone else's suffering, I can again see the politics. There's a guard hired by the university in order to keep the homeless out of the museum. Cecile's thinking of organizing a protest. I am encouraging. Cecile makes phone calls for advice and support while I supervise Colby's bath. He can turn the water off, but not on. I try not to make psychological inferences.

Cecile's politics float through the East Bay phone lines but collapse after she hugs Colby good night. His wet hair, dark and flat curls sticking to his head at impossible angles, is enough to make either of us maudlin.

"Promise me we'll never be homeless," she says.

"We won't," I say, knowing such reassurances are useless.

"Promise me we'll always have a nice place to live," Cecile demands extravangantly.

"What's nice?" I challenge. I suddenly don't want to soothe.

"I've had a hard day," Cecile says, "can't you just humor me?"

"No," I admit. I should tell her I've had a hard day too. I should tell her about the parking ticket. Maybe I will. In a minute.

I wait too long. Cecile is slamming out of the house, onto Alcatraz Street, out of our home. I wonder if she'll take the car.

I never understand why our arguments happen. Why I get stubborn. Why she gets angry. Sometimes it seems like it has more to do with the rest of the world than with either of us, than with both of us together.

I slip into Cecile's side of the bed. Maybe being over here will let me feel how she feels. I arrange my body as if I am her, half-sleeping. One arm over my head. I keep my eyes open, though. Her view looks the same as mine: seven inches closer to the window doesn't make much difference. The loyal tree in the tiny backyard doesn't seem any larger, or any smaller. I wait for Cecile to come home. I'll move over to my side of the bed when I hear her at the front door. Pretending I've never pretended to be her.

"More attempts to count the homeless in the census," Cecile reads aloud, interrupting herself to ask me if I'm packed.

I am. Haphazardly. Half-heartedly.

I hate being away from Colby. And Cecile.

I am supposed to be feeling lucky. I have an interview at one of the few schools in the country ready to teach philosophy to high school students. No masters degree required. I can even get a teaching certificate, with a few adjustments in my credentials. I can have a job.

I hate airplanes.

From the air, Berkeley and Oakland look lonely. I can't even imagine that I see Cecile and Colby. Banked against the mountains, the cities look forlorn, tenuous. Soon, there are the squares and circles of agri-business, looking like geometric Eisenhower-era linoleum, the little trucks like food specks trapped in the wax build-up. Then there's the snow of the Sierra Nevadas, brilliant but not beautiful.

The plane is probably above Utah when I want nothing more than to push myself through that small double-glassed window and dive into the blood-colored land. The openness of it, like an ocean that could be walked on. Its desolation is hypothetical from the air. Here, I could know freedom, joy. My visions would be clear. I could love this land like a lover, faithful forever. Like a mother, bodily connected. Here, I would be home.

I ask the flight attendent where we are. He doesn't know.

Two novels, one plane, and three snacks later, I land.

Home is what I had run away from. The unforgiving grit of it. The hazy confinement of it. I am hoping it has changed. Maybe the museums aren't still all uptown, but not too far up; maybe the queers aren't tossed next to boutiques with three-hundred-dollar shirts; maybe the streets aren't dirty, the men aren't agressive, the women aren't harried. Maybe this isn't the city I remember, the city I left, the city I've measured every other city against, as if it were some standard that could be escaped but not denied.

Or maybe I've changed. Maybe I'm less volatile, or more determined. I could even be less marginal, more mature. I have better clothes, a wallet with a credit card, cash for a taxi. I have an address for a hotel. I am here for a job interview. As a teacher. Respectable.

But the only thing about me that has really changed is my vocabulary. I have learned not to say *yeah*, or use *fuckin'* as an all-purpose adjective. And I have learned how to describe this place as a postmodernist construct. I can talk about fragmented polities, urban identities, terrains of semiotics.

Talking shit, even sophisticated shit, has its limits. I pluck my bag from the claim carousel, am passed through yet another security checkpoint, and pretend I know where the line of cabs will be, all in silence. The cab drivers are leaning on their cars not too far from where I thought they might be. They're all watching while a black man with a tattered knapsack yells at a white woman with a tattered knapsack. It's hard to tell if either is homeless; airports skew all clues. He is yelling *bitch, bitch, you bitch* at her.

"Welcome to New York," a man says to me. I recognize his suit, if not him, from my flight.

Welcome to the world.

None of the cab drivers seem interested in me. Everyone is interested in her. I am interested in her. She's a woman suffering a peculiarly female slander. Gender is my standard.

Until she screams, "Just get away from me, nigger." Then my spectator's sympathies slide, like those plastic glasses on those plastic airplane trays during turbulence. Loyalty has just become too expensive. I want a cab. I want to go home.

"Get your slut-ass home," he yells again. Not to me. To her.

I hurry into a cab before she says something else. Before the balance shifts again. I want my sexism clean; I want it uncomplicated.

Luckily, my cab driver doesn't speak English.

From the hotel, I call Cecile.

"Maybe this is good," she says, "a chance to confront the past."

I hate it when Cecile gets optimistic.

"Let me talk to Colby," I say. When I ask him if he misses me, he says, "Not really." I vow to teach him about the limits of honesty when I get back to California.

When I get back to California I am going to listen to Cecile read me the newspaper, the *Oakland Tribune*, or even the *San Francisco Chronicle*. When I get home I am going to read Colby five whole pages of *Animals And Where They Live* without skipping a single word. When

I get home I am going to sprawl across Cecile's side of the bed and try to read some book about feminist philosophy.

When I get home I am going to forget about the white woman and the black man. Forget their voices. But now they are in the small room with me. Like a memory.

Other women suppress incest memories. I had no man close enough to touch me. And my mother never did.

I suppress racial memories.

Once I was late coming home from Rosa's house. I ran the six blocks, past the lit street lights, past the twenty-four-hour factories that made cans from metal, seat covers from fabrics, furniture protectors from plastic. Up five flights of stairs. Into my mother's apartment.

There was a man chasing me. I got scared. I went the wrong way. I didn't want him to follow me home.

And then I added this detail: the man was black.

I don't remember now what reaction the added detail caused. There were lots of black men in my neighborhood. Rosa's father was black. My mother had dated a black man. What I remember is my shame at choosing that detail. At eleven, I knew what detail to choose to adorn the pursuing man, just as I knew that it was wrong to be late and more wrong to be late because I didn't notice it getting dark. Didn't notice it because my eyes were closed and I was kissing Rosa. I used what I knew about one thing to protect me from what I knew about something else.

Later, I added another detail. "Yeah, before the man chased me, he looked at his watch." My white mother and our Asian neighbor laughed, cruelly. I spent weeks trying to decide how they knew I was lying. Could they tell I'd been kissing? Was my path home too confusing? I wanted to confide in Rosa, but we did not spend our time alone talking.

Sitting in her kitchen one Saturday, I watched her father take off his watch to go to the factory. "Dangerous," he explained as if I had asked why, "it could get caught in the machinery. Pull a man's arm off," Rosa's father said, laughing.

My mother must have talked to Rosa's mother, I thought.

The high school is filled with the kind of kids I imagine that Rosa and I were. Except I didn't know Rosa in high school. Except I never really went to high school. How am I going to teach high school if I can't remember it? I ask myself. How am I going to teach when I have so much to learn?

During the interview, I am asked other questions:

"What are your theories of pedagogy?"

"What philosopher would you teach even though you don't want to?"

"What makes you think high school students should be taught philosophy?"

"How would you make philosophy relevant to kids who only want to get a job?"

"What makes you think we should hire you rather than the many Ph.D. candidates who have applied for this position?"

"How do you relate to kids from multicultural backgrounds?"

I can't answer any of the questions, but I respond. These teachers have a seriousness I somehow did not expect. They have a pilot program in philosophy. They have a target school and money from the state. They have a dedication I don't know if I have.

In the interview with the principal, he wants to know about my background. Would I be compassionate to kids from broken homes? That's a phrase I haven't heard for years and years. I try to display my compassion.

"Do you come from a broken home?" He asks the direct and unavoidable question. But does he mean my mother? Or does he mean me, as a lesbian mother?

"All homes are broken."

"Homeless activist Mitch Ryder commits suicide," Cecile reads from the *Oakland Tribune*. I don't ask how, why. I don't want to know.

It's something far away. The East Coast. Someone else's dream, someone else's nightmare. It's in Washington, D.C., which is not New York but not far enough away from New York to make a difference.

It is far enough away from here to make all the difference.

I belong in Berkeley.

Where I have six more weeks until I graduate with the worthless B.A. I have wanted for so long, buoyed by a teaching certificate that I'm finding out doesn't mean anything.

Where I don't have a job.

Where Cecile doesn't have a job. Terminated, not for organizing the protest, but because of university cutbacks. The protest, of course, helped the administration decide who should be fired from the library staff. Money was needed to hire an additional security guard.

"There's a candlelight vigil in People's Park tonight," Cecile tells me.

"Where do the homeless get the candles from?" I ask her.

"Donated," she explains, as if she knows. She might. She's been getting more and more active with the homeless. Next she'll be organizing a homeless art show.

At first, when I got back from New York, she asked me question after question. Like I was being interviewed all over again.

I keep telling her it is ugly.

Cecile, who is afraid of New York for its reputed violence, its vertical hugeness, its unredeemed snobbishness, does not think ugliness is fearsome.

She wants me to describe how it is ugly, as if ugliness were an object and not an emotion. I try to tell her about a pitiful plot of marigolds in Brooklyn, piss yellow and well-watered, dwarfed by the brick echoes of demanding voices. I try to tell her about highways where no cars move, about abandoned factories, about people yelling at each other.

"There must be trees," she argues.

"One or two," I admit. "But they lose their leaves in winter."

"That's not unnatural," she says. She knows that nature from books. As does Colby. In *Animals And Where They Live*, the seasons are explained, and how animals cope with the bare trees: they hibernate or they migrate.

"Maybe," I say, knowing there's nothing I can say. She hasn't seen those death sticks of winter. Neither has Colby. When I was a kid, I thought winter was everywhere; that everywhere was concrete. Now

I want the subtlety of seasons that replay themeselves daily. Now I want a splurge of variegated wildflowers, appearing for no reason in the western drought, needing neither attention nor admiration to survive.

"The ocean is there," Cecile tries again.

"Yeah," I say, again knowing there is nothing I can say. She knows the ocean from maps. She hasn't seen its dead brown foam, its swash of needles and cigarette butts.

"There are no earthquakes there," Cecile tries again.

"You fuckin' really want to leave this fuckin' place, don't you?" Maybe my vocabulary hasn't changed as much as I like to think.

"I think I could find a job there," Cecile says, simply.

Maybe we could go. Maybe I could teach those high school students Plato—the body as temporary home for the immortal soul. Or at least that's what Socrates says before he drinks the hemlock. Or have them read about homosexual love. I'd even do postmodernist stuff. Fragmented identities. Give them intellectual concepts for what they already know.

But the school does not call me.

It's embarrassing. The way Cecile waits for the phone to ring. The way the few friends I've made here keeping asking me, "Have you heard from New York yet?" I avoid the topic.

"You'd just love New York," my friend Nina tells me. We are drinking coffee in Berkeley. She is telling me about her privileged life on Long Island. "But it was never really my home, you know," she says.

I shake my head as if I do.

Then we talk about her therapy.

Was Mitch Ryder in therapy? I wonder.

Then we talk about her incest.

Was Mitch Ryder incested? I wonder.

Once I kicked my bike and announced, "I'm going to kill myself." I liked the violent drama of it. I didn't even care if my girlfriend was impressed; I had impressed myself. Later she would be impressed with other girlfriends, and one of them would kill herself. Drugs were an excuse for some of us, like marriage. Others were more direct. I liked to blame it on poverty.

But poverty was an excuse, too. Shannon was rich. The first rich girl I ever knew. She taught me that having a nice house didn't mean one couldn't be unhappy. We did spiritual experiments together. Tried to levitate glass balls and stuff like that. She later became a Maharishi groupie, and then a TM instructor. Her father paid for advanced guru instruction in Switzerland, then India. Looking back now, I think she was incested. I wonder if she left the Maharishi, if she's in therapy now, if she survived.

While I've been preoccupied with incest, Nina has accomplished a postmodern shift: we are talking about nature as a machine and machines as nature, about the spirit of plastic, and about all life as socially constructed.

Then our coffee is cold.

I walk the streets like I belong in Berkeley, where everyone looks posed as if in advertisement for hipness, even the homeless—especially the homeless. The homeless have their tans, have their puppies tied to their shopping carts, have tie-dyed bandanas looped around their puppies' necks. The homeless have their organizations, their volunteers, their Ceciles.

Cecile is at another meeting. I get Colby from school. Walk home. Decide to drive to a bookstore. My spirituality has degenerated into seeking mystical assistance in locating parking spaces. Convenience is secondary. I want time. Not giving quarters to the homeless is only part of the problem. We're also broke.

Too broke to buy books, but not too broke to look. To use the store like a library. To sit in a chair and browse by reading whole chapters. To stand in the women's section, but never more than an hour. Never too obvious. And never, money or not, to leaf through those books that bear subtitles like, *Heal The Inner Orphan And Begin The Journey Home*.

Cecile doesn't get home until after Colby is fed, bathed, read, and asleep. I would like to be angry with her. I would like to be resentful. Instead, I feel passionate.

I burrow my way into her as if I am a hermit crab and she is a perfect shell. Home. In our ocean of a bed. The tree outside our window bending toward a rare night rain.

In the morning, the tree looks at us wetly. My body clutches stiffly, not from last night's embraces but from the dampness. I can hear the fog horns in the distance, though the fog feels like it's in my head. Every morning is like this. The rain makes it only slightly more severe. The headaches. The nosebleeds. The limbs that won't bend. The pains that travel through the bones. It's the dampness.

It's the bay.

Nature betrays, but even if I were to become like a machine, I would be broken and rusted and in need of oil and attention. And these days, it is cheaper to replace than repair. Perhaps I should junk myself.

Suicide is always less of an option when there are things to do. I have to walk Colby to school.

He recites facts about the flowers we see. The same facts as yesterday morning. And the morning before that. But scattered among the flowers are lots of moving creatures. Snails of all sizes. Even more on the sidewalks. And covering the concrete stairs to Colby's school.

"Don't step on them," I warn.

The children collect themselves to inspect the snails. They categorize the biggest, the smallest, the fattest, the one with its antlers moving the most, the fastest. I've never seen so many slugs in shells.

"It's like the beach," one child says. I know that her name is Prapti and that she is from Iraq. A veiled and sneakered woman who could be her mother stands close to her, whispering in a language I do not understand.

"Snails do not live at the beach," Colby pronounces.

"Yes, they do." Prapti is undaunted. "That's why they have shells."

"You are wrong," Colby deepens his voice. My beautiful child, my constant companion. So stark Anglo-white in the morning fog, with blond hair, blue eyes, and a new jacket. An advertisement for America. My sweet dream, my perfect pleasure. So pompous minature male on the school steps, with rough elbows, growing testicles, and a Ninja Turtle backpack. An advertisement for Boyhood.

"I am not," Prapti insists. She is darker, smaller, female. She has all my sympathies. I should intervene for her. The racism here is clean, the sexism just as clean, dirtied only by my own flesh and blood. I want to be an impartial observer in these conflicts. I do not want to implicated. Why isn't this someone else's kid? Maybe Prapti can handle it by herself. She seems pretty strong. And isn't it adultist to interfere?

"You are," Colby says flatly. "The shells are their homes. They carry them everywhere."

"Well," I say, before Prapti can reply, "if the shells are homes they can take anywhere, then they can take them to the beach."

I smile at Prapti, expecting she'll compliment me like the students always compliment Socrates. She looks away.

I smile at the woman I think is Prapti's mother. She smiles back, then tells me, in English, that she cannot speak English.

"The snails always come out in the rain," another adult intrudes.

"That's right," Colby echoes. "Snails always come outside when it rains to drink the water." How does he know this? I wonder. And what makes him think he does?

"Not always," I say, just to be contrary.

"Oh, always," the adult says innocently.

Nothing is always. And is that why they come out, to drink? Or do they just slide better on the slick concrete? Or is it an omen, an augur, a sign of something?

I leave the kids on the steps and stretch my stiff bones down the hill. I'm not surprised to find Cecile at the door in a T-shirt, waiting for me, wearing her I-have-something-to-tell-you-smile.

"I'm home," I say simply, meaning it.

"I know," says Cecile. "I know."

East Of New York

"In Peru, October is earthquake month." Cecile is reading *Newsday* out loud while Colby pours cold milk on cold cereal in preparation for another day of first grade.

East of New York, October is avalanche month. Only it is pieces of trees rather than mountains that fall on our heads. There are no reports of fissures underground, of shifting, of the grinding roll the three of us remember from California. There is no talk of disaster. Everyone acts as if this strip-mining of leaves is natural. Some even act as if it is pleasurable.

Colby likes the colors of the leaves. He collects them on the way to the bus stop. And back. He wants me to admire his collection of leaves the way I have admired collections of feathers, collections of shells. He arranges them in his room. I throw them away. While cleaning. Accidentally. The feathers and shells and dust undisturbed.

Colby likes school. He runs to the bus stop in the morning. And back. He wants me to admire what he tells me he's learning the way I have admired his learning to read, to tell time. He recites a poem about Columbus Day. I scream.

"Do you think we discovered New York by moving here?"

"No," he answers.

"Why not?"

He looks at me as if I'm becoming someone he doesn't want to know. He answers me anyway. "Because there were people already living here."

"Exactly!" I shriek triumphantly. "Just like when Columbus drove his stupid boat across the ocean. There were people already here."

"Actually," Colby pauses for dramatic effect before he impresses me with his new-found knowledge, "there were three ships. And only Indians were already here."

I scream for Cecile, but she is already here. Sitting beside Colby. Remembering with him how we went to Navaho Nation and saw Window Rock. Remembering with him our discussions of the reservations and the United States government. Remembering with him our friend Sara who lives in Berkeley and who is Sioux.

Colby listens, seeming to remember. But I'm wondering how we can do anything other than totally confuse and alienate him. Even the best of alternative schools have not been alternative enough. And here, where alternative means private, we can't afford the counterculture. We can barely afford our rent.

The branches bang on the windows. Without leaves to soften the blows, the sound is harsh rather than mysterious. The summer rustle of sheets wet with sex is being replaced by the winter welting of flesh whipped by branches. The inside of our house seems haunted.

Outside is no better. The leaves form shallow but violent streams, intermixing the colors of blood, shit, piss. There is no downstream, no release. There is a flowing down the gutter, but then the blowing back in the face. Shards of leaves, styrofoam, cellophane, and indecipherable garbage spray toward the eyes. The wind grows cold and careless, like forgettable love.

October is inescapable, despite the calendar's even grids promising that time is marching on. I want to run, not march. To run back to California. Or run farther back in my own life to Florida beaches, and farther back in history to a time when those Florida beaches were not "developed." Or better yet, I'll run somewhere we've never been. Somewhere undiscovered.

I grab Cecile. I grab Colby. I make plans. I pack juice, nuts, cheese. I convince them into the car. I drive in the most ridiculous direction I can think of. Further north. Further east.

Salem, Massachusetts, on All Hallow's Eve.

"I think Colby needs to know these things," I explain.

"You're torturing yourself," Cecile sighs.

The instruments of torture are proudly displayed in the shopping mall areas. The instruments are wood. The absence of fire is palpable. It flicks around us and demands memory. The voices that haunt this place demand memory.

The voices are not shrill. Just insistent.

Like the voices we heard in a Wyoming canyon. Women screaming. Some sort of animal keening. "Jesus Christ," Cecile had muttered. We pulled off the side of the road, looking for a historical marker. Some commemoration of massacre. Some etching in metal to substantiate the voices. There wasn't any. It was all too ordinary. Only the voices demanded memory.

Colby's voice: "I wish those people would stop yelling." His matter-of-factness shocked us. We wanted to convince ourselves we were sharing an auditory hallucination, provoked by made-for-TV westerns or novels or cigarette advertisements. Then Colby spoke. And then we wanted to convince ourselves that even though we hadn't had a television set for years, and even though he couldn't read Zane Grey, Colby looked at those Marlboro billboards and absorbed history. But his voice joined the other voices demanding memory.

In Salem, the memories are documented with placards and plaques. The pillorying posts and stocks look benign even in twilight. People take pictures. People wear costumes. The whole town has been turned into a tourist trap based on the witch motif. Is it better to be co-opted or forgotten?

How do we teach Colby when we don't know ourselves? I marshall and memorize facts, phrases, images:

Once the land was thick with forest and the beaches shone with clams beating like hearts in smooth shells.

Once the women were strong with themselves and everyone listened when they said they heard spirits.

It was not so long ago.

And it was here. Right here, east of New York.

I place what I want him to know on his dinner plate, stir it in his food, sprinkle it like salt. Every dinner conversation Cecile and I are twin Penelopes, unraveling things people told him today. Saying, *No, Columbus did not discover America.* Saying, *No, witches don't eat children.* Wondering when he will bring home something we can't unravel. Or when he will learn to stop bringing things home to his mothers, those terrible invisible twins.

Somewhere, leaves are burning.

Winter Denial

So far, winter has brought us only dissonance. I hate winter with a silence severe enough to compete with the brush of snowflakes rubbing against one another for warmth. Colby loves winter with a boisterousness that only a seven-year old who has never seen snow or lost mittens can achieve. Cecile reverberates in the spaces between us, consoling and cajoling me, calming and quieting Colby. It is her first New York winter, her first winter.

She bounces back and forth between us, but mostly back and forth between us and her new job at the Women's Art Foundation of El Barrio/East Harlem. She's confusing English and Spanish, confusing the seasons, confusing me with Colby.

The last thing that needs to be added to such confusion is Colby learning to lie.

At first, the lies are flurries, drops of moisture that I can easily mistake for rain. One evening there is a crystalline shape so definite that even I can't deny it. Colby's guilt refracts and splinters as he snatches the backpack he'd said was empty. It isn't empty. It is filled with the gum I told him he could not take to school in his backpack. I throw the gum in the garbage.

"Cecile," I say, "I have to talk with you."

She nods her head as if it is very heavy. She says she is tired. Tired from another evening meeting. She lays on our bed "just to rest." She falls asleep. I tell her about the gum, the backpack, the guilt.

In a few days, there is the first accumulation, enough to be swept by the wind into little drifts. Colby says he doesn't know how his shirt got ripped, or his jeans. I'm afraid there is a bully at school, someone Colby is more afraid of than me. I decide to let the snow melt of its own accord.

"Cecile," I say, "you have to talk with Colby."

She nods her head as if it is very light. She says she is tired. Tired from riding the subways uptown/downtown/out-of-town. She falls asleep. I tell her about the rips, the jeans, the fear.

Then there is the blizzard.

My appointment with his teacher is in the late afternoon. I call Cecile and ask her to come home, but she has a meeting with a Nicaraguan lesbian scupltor that she can't miss. She doesn't ask me what I want. I leave work early. Getting home on the sanded salted roads and just wanting to eat. Anything. But nothing seems comforting enough.

Because what I want is someone to bring me a broad, painted plate of beautifully arranged edible colors, sweet and fresh, and undeniably tropical. Things I can't find in New York in winter. Or afford. And my someone isn't here to arrange anything on any kind of plate for me anyway.

I walk the few blocks to Colby's school. The cold makes my face hurt and my ears sting. I want to vomit or cry. Or both. The snow blinds. It melts wet down my back, sinking into my skin.

Colby's teacher is courteous. She knows I am a teacher too, but I tell her again. Just to make sure. Conversational details: high school, pilot program, challenging. Just to remove the edge of dykey difference. She smiles, confidentially. I smile, conspiratorially.

Deceitfully. Because I am already convinced that whatever Colby has done is not sufficient to warrant this parent-teacher conference in the middle of a blizzard, to merit this elementary school drama. I'm on his side. Irrevocably. Except if he's hit a girl. Or a woman. But Colby would never do that. He's told me he wouldn't.

What he hasn't told me is that he's been getting notes sent home. It seems he uses too much glue and sculpts little mountains of it rather than using it properly. I'm wishing my pregnant high school students had such profound problems. But it also seems like he loses too many things, like the first note home about the glue, and the second note home about the glue and losing the first note. The third note had a command: *Please sign and return.* This note wasn't lost. It was signed and was returned. And on the signature line, underneath the page of the teacher's precise cursive, the letters boldly spell CECILE, in Colby's most careful first-grade printing.

My first impulse is to laugh. It is such a pitiful attempt: how could he think he could forge Cecile's signature? My next impulse is to blame. It is such a brazen act: how could he have thought of something like that by himself? Then I begin to cope. It is such a dangerous betrayal: how could he have done something like that to us?

"I'll take care of it," I tell Colby's teacher.

"I knew you would." She is still exuding confidence, although now it is mixed with something that might be compassion.

Colby is waiting for me in the school lunchroom. Instead of his usual spontaneous smile, I'm looking at the most self-conscious attempt at normality I've ever seen.

"Come on."

His winter coat. His winter boots. His second pair of mittens. His hat.

The walk home. The snow is as silent as us.

"You know what your teacher told me. I'm going to think about it for a little while, and then we're going to talk. First, you can do your homework."

I need to think about this. I need to think about it with Cecile. There is no answer at the El Barrio office. I want to run all over New York looking for her until I find her. And then I want to run away with her, away from winter.

"Isn't there anything at all you like about winter?" Cecile had asked me last week, hopefully. We were walking down East 116th Street, outside the Women's Art Foundation office. It was Saturday. Colby and I had brought Cecile lunch, and we were going to the Ponce to get coffee con leche. It was snowing, casually. Colby was planning for the first really big snow, how he would make snowmen. "Snow persons," I had corrected him, and he had dutifully echoed.

"Not really," I had answered Cecile. She'd gone back to work then, not even waiting for her coffee.

Later, walking around Manhattan with Colby, missing Cecile, I thought of something I liked about winter: all the women look like dykes. With their high boots, wide-coated shoulders, with their feet planted firmly on the slippery ground, they walk aggressively against the winter wind. They cross the street like dykes, striding rather than skipping, dressed darkly and competently. And when it snows, they look into each other's faces like dykes, comfortable with sharing the same fate, yet more wary than friendly to strangers.

I meant to tell Cecile this discovery. That what I liked about winter was that all the women looked like dykes, except she didn't come home until I was asleep that Saturday night. Except I thought she might say that all the women in winter looked like dykes except me.

I'm not into dykedom. I'm into denial.

My best boots are sneakers. Canvas. Low tops. Or the purple loafers I wore to the parent-teacher conference. Or the kind of black flat round shoes I usually wear to work. I skid and slip when I walk.

My warmest jacket is silk and fuchsia and bought on sale in San Francisco's Chinatown. I explain to Cecile that the cotton padding keeps me toastier than any down-filled parka, any virgin wool, any fur skin banned by our politics. I pretend Cecile believes me.

What I cannot pretend is that I belong in any winter wonderland. I am simply not blonde enough. And I cannot belong in winter because winter does not belong to me. It belongs to all those women in their lined boots and expensive coats, the women who look like dykes but aren't.

The winter belongs to those who can appreciate white snow without automatically picturing it absorbing drops of blood, perfect red dots that spread and lighten into a beautiful, blurry pink, until another blot darkens them again, until the circles merge and curl and overlap, until it seems the blood could burrow to the frozen dirt silent beneath the white. The winter belongs to those who can walk briskly to keep warm without thinking their survival depends on it, who know they will reach a warm home, who have never burned broken pieces of furniture to keep warm, who have never burned their tongue sipping water boiled on a hot plate.

The winter belongs to those who have not been owned by the winter. By those who have not been owned.

I learned about ownership in grade school one winter, but the teachers lied and taught us that it was abolished. I learned to recite the Gettysburg Address for Lincoln's birthday. Our class performed for the assembly. I wore a plaid dress that my mother was very proud of making and knee socks that I held above my shins with rubber bands that left cold and itchy indentations in my flesh. After our recitation, our class heard about a great war where a lot of men who were related to each other killed each other. This was supposed to be a huge tragedy, but it reminded us of our neighborhoods.

The really important part, though, was that this terrible war had made us all free. The emphasis was on the all. The principal lectured: This war freed the previously enslaved Blacks. I watched Candy and Ann etch both gratitude and suffering on their faces, as I tried to emulate pride and compassion. The principal preached: No one could own anyone else now. We congratulated ourselves on our past. Slavery is still acceptable in parts of Africa. Candy and Ann shifted their faces into expressions of shameful complicity as I tried to maintain my forced emulation of compassionate pride. We must take pride in our forefathers who guaranteed us all our precious liberties, in a country where no man may own another. We applauded because it was over and that was what we were trained to do.

But not one of us, not Candy or Ann or me or even stupid Timothy Spandex, walked out of that assembly, out of that asbestos-lined brick school, out into the February slush that could be frozen by the approaching darkness, as if we were not owned.

We were owned by our parents, or the adults who fed and kept us. And they were owned by the landlords, by the factories or the welfare ladies, by the salesclerks at Ginsburg's or Brown's or O'Donnell's or wherever we shopped for food or clothes or shoes, the salesclerks who could be nice or rude depending on the mood of the winter sky or how successful we were in not dripping on their floors or how much credit we needed.

We were not just owned by poverty; we were owned by the past. But not just one past. It would have been easy to have been owned by the glorious past of a glorious war that made all men free, forgetting even that the women weren't made anything except women. Instead, we were owned by many pasts: the pasts of our mothers and the fantastic pasts of those men who might have been our fathers; the pasts of our neighbors who had God-only-knows-why left their superior-in-every-way birthplace that they variously called Italy, Poland, The South, China, Back Home, My Country; the pasts the adults who cared for us might have had if only we hadn't have been born.

And we were owned by our own lies and the lies we believed even when we knew they were lies. We pretended we were not owned. We pretended that if we worked very hard and very long and were always very honest, we would not be owned.

I grew up believing it was important to be honest, probably more important that not being lazy, and certainly more important than not being messy with glue. Maybe it's the way I grew up, or maybe something else, but I want Colby to be honest, especially honest with me. I want our relationship not to be one of ownership of child by parent, but something I don't know what else to call but honesty.

And if I'm honest, I want him to be perfect so that no one can blame anything on his dyke parentage.

I redial Cecile. No answer.

Cecile is my lover. My beloved. She is usually grumpy, often impatient, sometimes insecure, and always sexy. She's loyal, honest, and good with maps. She gets on my nerves and takes care of me when I need taking care of. She's afraid of rattlesnakes and has the world's most expressive eyebrows. She's Colby's co-mother. Where the hell is she?

Colby and I sit on his bed. Without touching.

"Tell me about it," I say.

He shrugs.

"O.K. Sit here until you think of what to say."

I redial Cecile. Where the fuck is she? I leaf through the address book. None of these numbers will connect me to Cecile. All of these numbers multiply the ways she is being denied to me.

"I'm sorry," Colby cries out.

"That's it? That's all you can say?"

He shrugs.

I'm on the edge of anger, but I recognize that silence from my own childhood. It is anything but the arrogance and stubbornness that provoked such accusations from my mother. It is scared. It is a holding still so that the world doesn't split and shatter.

It is its own punishment.

But before I speak about punishment, I will think about it some more. I have given up talking to Cecile about it.

"Get ready for bed."

Colby looks at me, almost gratefully.

When Cecile comes home, it is later than late. Colby is asleep. I am cold. It is snowing.

I unlatch the double safety locks for her. She has a paper bag. I don't care. I go to bed. Our bed.

She takes too long to join me.

"What's up," she says, finally.

I am cold. Silent. The snow is shadowless in the streetlight outside our bedroom window.

"Why don't you tell me what's up?" she coaxes.

"Colby has been lying to us," I tell her. "For weeks," I add for emphasis.

"Why didn't you tell me?" she asks.

"I did," I say.

For a second, I think she is going to protest. I am prepared to argue. I did tell her. Even if she was sleeping. It wasn't my not telling her that prevented her from not hearing. I'm still expecting the coolness of denial to rush from her. But then I remember that she is Cecile.

Cecile, sitting on the bed, looking like a dyke even without the bulk of a coat or the toughness of boots. Looking tired, exhausted even.

"Want any?" she asks.

And on the night table is a plate of cut color. Tropical and lush. Mango. Avocado. Papaya. Akee. Kiwi.

Kissing Doesn't Kill

"Kiss me," Cecile commands. She is standing against the bedroom door in her underpants and a ripped undershirt. The Saturday morning sun—which slants at its unique Saturday angle—pierces the cracks in the bamboo window shade and refracts off the pink wall. I can hear Cecile's soft breathing. I can hear seven-year-old Colby's snorts of sleep in the next room. I can hear my own heart.

"Not unless you come back to bed," I reply.

"What's the matter, don't you like standing-up sex?"

"Cecile, don't be gross."

"What's gross about it?" Cecile asks, laughing.

"My knees," I laugh back. "My knees would be totally gross if we did that."

"Totally gross?" Cecile echoes.

"Hey, I teach teenagers. What can I say?"

"You can say you remember when your knees were stronger and how you used to lean against me."

"You and the wall," I correct.

"You used to throw me to the floor with passion."

"Until I hit my head on the chair leg and saw stars for weeks."

"You used to see stars all the time."

If I didn't know Cecile so long and so deep, I'd think she was complaining. She isn't. She's tracing our romance. Soon she will slide next to me with her coffee cup and mine, and ask me if I remember the first time we ever made love. What we remember is not the first time, but the accumulation of memories of the first time. We reinscribe it in our memories with our words. Then we will relive it, not as reenactment, but as reinvention. With Cecile, every time is different.

This morning's love is intense. The mouth, the tongue, the body, blur and re-blur. I am chalky, pastel. I am crying. Sobbing, really.

Cecile is the one who should be crying, not me. I should be comforting her, holding her, allowing her to think about Estela. Estela, a Chilean artist whose work Cecile was close to placing with a new feminist art gallery downtown. Estela, dead. Visiting her mother and sister in Santiago. Everyone suspects the government, although which one is uncertain.

I only met Estela once. At dinner. She sat next to Colby and talked with him. So many adults ignore him, but she talked with him about the colors of clothes splashed around the table. Her fingers had a stubby beauty as they pointed. They crossed and recrossed as she and Colby compared the numerous shades of purple. They laughed. Her fingers could laugh.

The death of that laughter could make me cry for weeks.

But our weeks are not for crying; they are for work. For Cecile, there is the work of representing lesbian artists from South America. For Colby, there is the work of trying to survive in a New York public elementary school and maybe even learn something that nourishes love instead of narrowness. For me, there is the work of trying to survive in a New York public high school and maybe even teach something that encourages the risk of expansiveness instead of hate.

I'm teaching philosophy to high school students in a special pilot program. Eight classes of twenty students each, each class twice a week. I am really a teacher now, something I never thought I'd survive to do. Teaching kids who are a lot like I was. And a lot like I wasn't.

At least once every other week, and sometimes twice, a student will make an appointment to see me about "something really important." Her fourteen-fifteen-sixteen-year-old face is shining, womanly, but she looks more like Colby than Cecile. She glows with innocence, but she is also cynical, slick, and yes, sexy. The same way I was at fourteen-fifteen-sixteen. In fact, every one of these creatures I call young women remind me of myself: no matter that I wasn't Asian or Black, that I didn't streak my hair purple or wear bracelets from Guatemala, that I wouldn't talk to a teacher unless I had to, never mind sit in her office and tell her I was in love with her. The more sophisticated students talk about strong attractions and feelings that can't be denied and something that isn't just a crush.

I thank them for sharing their feelings. I am not at all grateful.

The bolder (and less sophisticated) students ask about my feelings for them. They want me to say that I love them. I would never say this. Not because I don't love them, but because the them that I love is the me that I was. I love them only as mirrors that would allow me to love myself like I never did. And because the them that I love is ephemeral. I love them only as girls who might grow to love themselves as women.

And because I don't love them, not really. Not as individuals. Sure, teaching is a lot like being in love, but with no one in particular. And for me, love is Cecile. I don't tell them I have been loving the same woman since they were in third grade.

Because I want to take them seriously. Because I want to tell them that they are worth loving. I don't tell them about transference or role models or the difficulties of coming out. I don't tell them to find a nice girl their own age or even suggest that they direct their attentions to their best friends, Claudia and Ernestine, who were in my office confessing love just last week. I want to take them seriously.

I say thank you and nothing else.

To anyone.

Not even to Cecile.

Especially not to Yvette, a co-teacher who comments on the line of girls that sometimes snakes by my office door.

"I'm role-modeling," I joke to Yvette.

"More like making all the girls at this school into lesbians," Yvette grumbles. Maybe she is just jealous that she doesn't have a line of girls, or even an office with a door. The office is part of the pilot program's perks, but I'm not sure it's worth it.

Yvette doesn't wear the crooked smile of envy. She is not smiling. I turn away and look back at her. She still is not smiling.

I close the door to my office. I am more innocent than any of my students. Despite the violence that has been my life, I never really expect people to be mean. Grumpy, yes, but not humorlessly mean. I should walk back to Yvette. I should tell her that I am not making anybody into anything, tell her these girls are as much lesbians as I was at their age. Don't tell her about current debates about sexual identity formation. Tell her I don't know why she hates me. Accuse her of being closeted or latent.

But I am not that innocent.

And she isn't the only one. And she isn't even among my private suspects for what comes to be known as the poster-burning incident. It's my poster, given to me by an admiring student. KISSING DOESN'T KILL: GREED AND INDIFFERENCE DO. By the Gran Fury Collective. Political art marking AIDS as a political crisis. Interracial and intersexed. Appearing on public buses in New York. And appearing in a public school hallway outside my office. My favorite part is the women's hairstyles.

It's the women who are burned off. KILL THE QUEERS is black magic-markered across the remains, including the kissing couple of a black man and white women. There are different sorts of accuracy.

The students in philosophy want to talk about the poster burning. I've scheduled us to talk about Foucault. Sometimes I think that they see philosophy as current events, or their feelings, or just gossip. Sometimes I wonder if I've gone overboard with my message that philosophy is accessible. Sometimes I want to know if they're as unfocused in their other classes, but I'm vulnerable in my pilot project and can't/won't/don't ask other teachers.

So, I try to make connections, try to surface assumptions. There is not a complete contradiction between rambling discussions and disciplined inquiries. And I try to cover the material, for the school administration cares less about discussion or discipline than measurable achievements. After this pilot program, the students should be able to to name the names of philosophy: to know who Plato is and when he lived, to be able to correctly identify postmodernism from four reductive multiple choices. To score better on the statewide Regents exam.

"Let's think about what Foucault might have said about the destruction of the poster," I say. "He died of AIDS." I add some poignant gossip.

My students do not succumb to my attempt. This is my favorite class of twenty: they are bright, articulate, culturally and politically mixed, and usually respectful. Sometimes they even do the assigned reading. But today they want to talk about me.

The student is white. Female. Sincere. Apparently heterosexual. She has never been in my office swearing undying love. She asks me, in front of the class, whether I feel threatened.

She wants me to bleed. To slash my flesh and bleed so that she can inspect my blood to see if it is really red.

I am vulnerable.

Ridiculous. She is sixteen, at most. I am one of the few out lesbians she knows. Maybe the only one. Certainly the only one teaching at this school. And it was my poster.

So, I answer her—her and the other nineteen teenagers in the classroom—being careful not to look at any one person in particular, especially not Claudia or Ernestine. I clothe my answer in the purples of untaught history, talk about lesbians burned as witches, or as criminals, or both. I clothe my answer in the purples of my own history, talk about being cornered by boys yelling dyke and throwing sharp rocks. I even manage to mention Foucault.

"You must feel really vulnerable," the white sincere young woman says.

She doesn't see how tough I am to have survived.

"We are all vulnerable," I say, trying to imagine how this young woman could not walk down the same streets near the high school as I do. "If we are lesbians or gay men, we are attacked on the street for being queer. If we are women, we are attacked on the streets and in our houses for being female. If we are African-American or Spanish or Asian, we are attacked for being not-white-enough. If we think we belong only in certain places at certain times and with our own kind, then we are vulnerable. And all of us are vulnerable."

I think my speech has all the right shades of pathos and passion. Maybe it can be a segue into Foucault's theory of power in the next class.

None of my students compliment me on my comments. No one comes that week to confess love, or even strong attraction. The hall outside my office feels strangely silent. I write the principal a memo about the incident in which I suggest/demand an investigation. I am very careful to straddle the slash between suggest and demand. I give copies to all my fellow teachers. The principal never replies. None of the other teachers talk to me about it except Yvette, who smiles as she says, "You've caused a lot of trouble, haven't you?"

When the war starts, it is another thing not to talk about. Yvette wears a flag pin on her daily dress. Soon, it nests in a yellow bow. The other teachers are like mirrors. Someone official orders yellow ribbons tied to the fence around the school. I start carrying Cecile's pocket knife, slashing the strips of cloth, watching them float toward the piles of garbage that fertilize the fence. I see Yvette watch me and my knife. She stands against the fence smoking a cigarette, those cancerous substitutes for kisses. The students want to talk about the war in class. They have relatives "over there in the Gulf." Brothers. Uncles. A few aunts and sisters. Lots of cousins. I lecture on Foucault. "This will be on the test," I say. *Support our troops,* the students say with the buttons on their jackets.

Colby's button says, *War is not good for children and other living things.* A child in his school rips it off his backpack and then spits on him. "He's just a jerk," Colby says. But he doesn't wear any more buttons.

Cecile threatens to kill the kid that spit on Colby.

"That will solve everything," I say.

We listen to the radio. It is our TV substitute. It is sufficient to provoke.

"What are you, a fuckin' third-grader?" I yell back at some general in some press conference.

"What's wrong with third-graders?" Colby wants to know.

"Wasn't that kid who spit on you in third grade?"

"No, he's a fourth-grader," Colby corrects.

"Well," I calm a bit, "I guess I'm just trying to say that these men should be acting like grownups rather than kids."

"Kids don't have bombs," Colby corrects again.

"Finish your breakfast, get ready for school, and come kiss me good-bye."

The ones with bombs drop them on Iraq at night.

Somewhere in Iraq there are two lesbians, holding onto each other in the darkness. Kissing. Kissing. Kissing as if their lives depend on it.

Cecile tells me to stop imagining things. "Besides," she says, "lesbians aren't allowed over there."

"Cecile," I yell at her louder than I did at the general, "what are you talking about? Have you forgotten Estela? Do you think they allow lesbians in Chile? Goddamn it, Cecile, you think they allow lesbians over here? In New York?"

"Look," Cecile says, "I just don't want to think about it. She turns the radio station.

To my favorite station instead of hers, like an apology. Yet the (post)-modern rock I usually find so soothing (the jarring chords cannot compete with its failure to remind me of the songs before Cecile) is being interrupted by news bulletins and commentaries on news bulletins.

And they are saying *We*, as in, *We are bombing Iraq*.

It's more than enough to make me long for the songs before Cecile. *It ain't me babe*. Where's Bob Dylan when we need him? Joan Baez? Hell, where's Buffy Saint-Marie?

And they are saying that they've made arrangements with a chain of florists to provide all the station listeners with yellow ribbons for our houses and cars.

I spin the radio dial, searching for what is now called classic rock. They're playing Rod Stewart.

We scatter numbers across the FM-band. Then the war ends.

They/we won.

It was tidy, and Americans are happy. It was expensive but hardly anyone talks on the radio about that. The country is in a recession. People continue to die of AIDS. New York City is laying off teachers.

The forsythia bloom, but they are yellow.

"Cecile," I say, "I'm losing my job."

"Kiss me," she says.

"Cecile," I say, "I'm being fired. There are other teachers hired the same time as me, but they're staying."

"Kiss me," she says.

"Cecile," I say, "you don't understand. I'm losing my job. We can't live on your salary. And I don't want Colby to grow up in this stupid country."

"You're right," Cecile says. "Let's move to Australia."

"That won't solve anything," I say. But I've always wanted to drive across that continent. Now might be the time to do it. "Besides," I add, "I don't know where we'll get the money."

Cecile laughs.

"Kiss me," I say.

Our laugh is so deep and so long that I know I will never kill or be killed. And maybe I will never die.

And maybe we will go to Australia.

Other titles from Firebrand Books include:

Artemis In Echo Park, Poetry by Eloise Klein Healy/$8.95

Beneath My Heart, Poetry by Janice Gould/$8.95

The Big Mama Stories by Shay Youngblood/$8.95

A Burst Of Light, Essays by Audre Lorde/$7.95

Crime Against Nature, Poetry by Minnie Bruce Pratt/$8.95

Diamonds Are A Dyke's Best Friend by Yvonne Zipter/$9.95

Dykes To Watch Out For, Cartoons by Alison Bechdel/$6.95

Exile In The Promised Land, A Memoir by Marcia Freedman/$8.95

Eye Of A Hurricane, Stories by Ruthann Robson/$8.95

The Fires Of Bride, A Novel by Ellen Galford/$8.95

Food & Spirits, Stories by Beth Brant (*Degonwadonti*)/$8.95

Free Ride, A Novel by Marilyn Gayle/$9.95

A Gathering Of Spirit, A Collection by North American Indian Women edited by Beth Brant (*Degonwadonti*)/$9.95

Getting Home Alive by Aurora Levins Morales and Rosario Morales /$8.95

The Gilda Stories, A Novel by Jewelle Gomez/$9.95

Good Enough To Eat, A Novel by Lesléa Newman/$8.95

Humid Pitch, Narrative Poetry by Cheryl Clarke/$8.95

Jewish Women's Call For Peace edited by Rita Falbel, Irena Klepfisz, and Donna Nevel/$4.95

Jonestown & Other Madness, Poetry by Pat Parker/$7.95

Just Say Yes, A Novel by Judith McDaniel/$8.95

The Land Of Look Behind, Prose and Poetry by Michelle Cliff/$6.95

A Letter To Harvey Milk, Short Stories by Lesléa Newman/$8.95

Letting In The Night, A Novel by Joan Lindau/$8.95

Living As A Lesbian, Poetry by Cheryl Clarke/$7.95

Making It, A Woman's Guide to Sex in the Age of AIDS by Cindy Patton and Janis Kelly/$4.95

Metamorphosis, Reflections On Recovery by Judith McDaniel/$7.95

Mohawk Trail by Beth Brant (*Degonwadonti*)/$7.95

Moll Cutpurse, A Novel by Ellen Galford/$7.95

More Dykes To Watch Out For, Cartoons by Alison Bechdel/$7.95

The Monarchs Are Flying, A Novel by Marion Foster/$8.95

Movement In Black, Poetry by Pat Parker/$8.95

My Mama's Dead Squirrel, Lesbian Essays on Southern Culture by Mab Segrest/$8.95

New, Improved! Dykes To Watch Out For, Cartoons by Alison Bechdel /$7.95

The Other Sappho, A Novel by Ellen Frye/$8.95

Out In The World, International Lesbian Organizing by Shelley Anderson/$4.95

Politics Of The Heart, A Lesbian Parenting Anthology edited by Sandra Pollack and Jeanne Vaughn/$11.95

Presenting. . . Sister NoBlues by Hattie Gossett/$8.95

Rebellion, Essays 1980-1991 by Minnie Bruce Pratt/$10.95

A Restricted Country by Joan Nestle/$8.95

Sacred Space by Geraldine Hatch Hanon/$9.95

Sanctuary, A Journey by Judith McDaniel/$7.95

Sans Souci, And Other Stories by Dionne Brand/$8.95

Scuttlebutt, A Novel by Jana Williams/$8.95

Shoulders, A Novel by Georgia Cotrell/$8.95

Simple Songs, Stories by Vickie Sears/$8.95

The Sun Is Not Merciful, Short Stories by Anna Lee Walters/$7.95

Tender Warriors, A Novel by Rachel Guido deVries/$8.95

This Is About Incest by Margaret Randall/$8.95

The Threshing Floor, Short Stories by Barbara Burford/$7.95

Trash, Stories by Dorothy Allison/$8.95

The Women Who Hate Me, Poetry by Dorothy Allison/$8.95

Words To The Wise, A Writer's Guide to Feminist and Lesbian Periodicals & Publishers by Andrea Fleck Clardy/$4.95

Yours In Struggle, Three Feminist Perspectives on Anti-Semitism and Racism by Elly Bulkin, Minnie Bruce Pratt, and Barbara Smith /$8.95

You can buy Firebrand titles at your bookstore, or order them directly from the publisher (141 The Commons, Ithaca, New York 14850, 607-272-0000).

Please include $2.00 shipping for the first book and $.50 for each additional book.

A free catalog is available on request.